Jillian Spectre
Dream Weaver

The Adventures of Jillian Spectre

NIC TATANO

Harper impulse
we've got the love

Harper*Impulse* an imprint of
HarperCollins*Publishers* Ltd
1 London Bridge Street
London SE1 9GF

www.harpercollins.co.uk

A Paperback Original 2015

First published in Great Britain in ebook format by Harper*Impulse* 2015

A catalogue record for this book is
available from the British Library

ISBN: 9780008140960

Automatically produced by Atomik ePublisher from Easypress

Printed and bound in Great Britain

For Myra, who turns dreams into reality...

Chapter 1

When you graduate from high school, you're often told you can change the world.

In my case, well... been there, done that.

But when you're an eighteen year old mystic seer who can physically be in two places at once and, oh yeah, you have what might be considered supernatural healing powers and an actual angel from Heaven on speed dial, saving the world is sort of an obligation. So instead of simply being Jillian Spectre, college freshman majoring in the ever popular *undecided*, I'm moonlighting as a comic book character. Boring classes that require regurgitation by day, redhead superheroine by night. No mask, no costume, no secret underground lair; just a freckled hundred and fifteen pound girl … and saving the planet is not above my pay grade.

So when my cellular version of the bat phone rings, and I see who's calling—

"Jillian, my partner's been shot! I need you right now!" says Detective Spencer Ball, NYPD's astral projection investigator and my occasional partner.

I know the routine. "Mom, I'll be right back!" I yell in the direction of the kitchen, as I stretch out on our living room couch, put the phone on speaker and close my eyes. Spencer, affectionately known as Fuzzball, quickly recites his hypnotic relaxation technique, making me relax and focus on his location as he describes the scene and the person in need of help.

And that person will die in minutes without me. I can hear the fear and concern in the detective's voice.

I create the scene in my mind and, in a blink, I'm there. In a moonlit alley somewhere in Manhattan.

The massive pool of blood on the ground and the twitching man make me jump back. It's one thing to have the detective tell you about it, another to actually see it.

"Jillian, hurry!" says Fuzzball, who is kneeling down next to his partner, pressing his hand over the guy's chest as blood oozes out.

I crouch down on the cool pavement next to his partner, a lean, dark haired man in his thirties whose dark eyes are flickering. "What's his name?"

"Jim." He turns to his partner. "Jimbo, she's here to help. Hang in there, buddy."

I take the dying man's trembling hand as he is gasping for air like a fish yanked out of the water. "Jim, look at me."

The man turns his head and locks eyes with me. His are deep pools of fear. I hear gurgling coming from his throat as he tries to talk and see blood trickle out of his mouth.

He knows he's going to die.

I tighten my grip on his hand. "You're going to be all right," I say.

He bites his lower lip as a single tear rolls down the side of his face. "Spence, tell my wife—" His voice is a whisper, barely audible.

"Hang in there!" says Fuzzball, grabbing Jim's face with his free hand and turning it so that he's facing me. "Now, Jillian!"

I close my eyes, see the dying man in my mind, and send as much of my life force as I can into him in one incredible rush. I see the blood flow stopping, the bullet working its way out, the wound beginning to heal, his breathing returning to normal, calm returning to his eyes—

And then I black out.

I'm holding a different hand and my hair is gently being stroked when I wake up. I already know the touch before I open my eyes.

I look up and see my boyfriend Ryan. I'm back on the couch with my head and shoulders on his lap. "Welcome back, Sparks." He leans down and kisses me on the forehead.

"Did I save him?"

Ryan flashes a big smile. "Yeah. Fuzzball called. Doctors at the hospital say they can't explain it but he's going to make a full recovery. Guess they don't study redheaded guardian angels with healing powers in med school."

I start to sit up but a throbbing headache pushes me back down and I grab my forehead. "Whoa. How long was I out?"

"Three hours."

"Wow. It's been a while since healing knocked me out. I thought I was past that. Damn, I'm fried."

"You should be. The guy was as close to death as anyone you ever saved."

"Yeah, no kidding. I've never seen anything like that. It was like a scene out of a gory movie. Good thing tomorrow's a Saturday so I can rest up." I reach up to run my fingers through his thick dark hair and let myself get lost in his deep blue eyes.

"Well, hate to tell you this, but we don't have the day off."

"What do you mean?"

My mom walks into the living room and smiles at me. "Good, you're up. You feelin' okay, sweetie?"

"My head feels like there's a man inside banging a Chinese gong, but I'll live. What's this about not having tomorrow off?"

Her smile disappears as she turns to Ryan. "You didn't tell her?"

"She just woke up, Mrs. Spectre. Didn't have a chance."

"Tell me what?"

She turns back to me with a familiar look that tells me something is very wrong. She bites her lower lip, then exhales. "We need to go to The Summit. Sebastien called."

Uh-oh. An emergency trip to the home office for those with

paranormal powers. This can't be good. "Yeah? And?"

"There's been a change with your father."

So it turns out my father, the deadbeat dad who abandoned me and mom when I was a year old, the guy who tried to turn society into a bunch of pod people with a mind controlling cell phone and now has a day job as a comatose villain, has taken a turn.

For better or worse, we don't know. Although worse wouldn't break my heart considering he nearly killed my boyfriend and best friend. But something tells me if that were the case, we wouldn't have been summoned to western New Jersey by Sebastien, head of The Council. The old guy in charge of monitoring everyone with paranormal powers doesn't mess around.

Sebastien leads me, Ryan and Mom into the antiseptic secure chamber. It's become my father's permanent home since we basically fried his brain and his ability to meld with technology by using a powerful computer virus provided by your tax dollars and Fuzzball's Man in Black buddy who works for the feds. He's still in a coma, face drawn, skin lacking in color, oblivious to the rest of the world. Nothing's changed since that day in May, the last time I saw him.

Well, nothing had changed until yesterday, according to Sebastien.

"So, what happened?" I ask, looking at my father through the glass. "He looks the same."

"His brain waves changed slightly," says Sebastien, as he stares at my father's body. "We monitor the activity constantly and last night something happened that we cannot explain."

"Is he waking up?" asks Mom, staring at the man who was once the love of her life before turning into an evil maniac. Her tense face tells me she's still conflicted, still wondering if we shorted out the evil part of his brain and the good man might be inside.

Sebastien shakes his head. "No. But we detected a change in his Delta waves. Jillian, you know the implications of that."

I nod. "Yeah. The brain waves of the subconscious. How he was going to control me with the phone. So, could he simply be dreaming?"

"Our experts don't think so. There was no rapid eye movement detected, and dreams would produce a different kind of brain wave pattern that we've seen before from him. The change in his pattern is not unlike what we saw when you combined yours with Ryan and Roxanne. Our theory is that... well, the simplest way to put it is that we think he's been contacted."

Ryan furrows his brow. "How is that even possible?"

Sebastien shakes his head. "We don't know," he says, then turns to Ryan. "Which is why I asked you to come along. We were hoping..."

"You want me to read his mind?" asks Ryan.

"No!" I yell, throwing out one arm in front of Ryan before Sebastien has the chance to answer. "My father almost killed him twice, and you want to risk his life over some brain wave change? Find another way."

"There is no danger," says Sebastien.

My blood pressure spikes. "How the hell can you be sure of that?"

Mom grabs my arm. "Young lady, watch your tone. Don't yell at Sebastien."

"I'll yell if he's going to risk my boyfriend's life."

"We know there's no danger because we already tried using other mind readers. None of them suffered any after effects," says Sebastien. "But they also got no results."

"Then why do you need me?" asks Ryan. "I just finished my apprenticeship. I'm sure the people you've got here are the best and have a lot more experience."

"You've made contact with him before," says Sebastien.

"There's another part to that equation," I say. "My father also went into *his* mind, remember?"

Sebastien ignores my comment and keeps looking at Ryan. "We feel you may experience different results because of your previous connection with Jillian and Roxanne. Your powers are slightly different than the average mind reader."

"What are you talking about?" asks Mom.

Sebastien looks at the ground. "I admit, I should have told you this before. But when the three of them connected it took his powers in a slightly different direction. Roxanne's as well. They are both more finely attuned, as if they somehow absorbed some of Jillian's incredible gifts."

"I don't care if he's the best mind reader on the planet," I say, folding my arms. "He's not doing it. End of story."

Ryan rests his hand on my shoulder. "Hang on a minute, Sparks. The two times he attacked me he sent his own thoughts. He can't do that now."

"You don't know that!" I say.

"Yes, we do," says Sebastien. "There is no risk. But it is up to you, Ryan. I certainly understand if you don't want to do this."

Ryan nods, and I can tell he wants to do it.

Damn friggin' testosterone. That rampant Y chromosome needs a leash.

I reach for Ryan's hand and tangle my fingers in his, then give him the most soulful look I can muster. "Please don't. You're not bulletproof."

"I'll be fine, Sparks," he says, smiling. "Besides, you're here to heal me if anything goes wrong. You've done it before. Twice."

Damn friggin' logic. Why am I in love with the only eighteen year old guy on the planet with a forty year old brain?

Ryan turns to Sebastien. "You want me to do this now?"

He nods. "The sooner we find out, the better."

"Okay." Ryan closes his eyes, which is what he does when he's about to read a mind. I squeeze his hand harder and he squeezes back.

My heart slams against my chest and I focus on him, ready to send as much healing energy as I can muster. But thankfully nothing happens.

Finally, after what seems like an eternity but is actually about sixty seconds, he opens his eyes and looks at me. "See, I'm fine."

My heart downshifts as I wrap my arms around his waist and lean my head on his chest.

"Did you get anything?" asks Sebastien.

Ryan nods as he puts an arm around my shoulder and pulls me closer, then kisses the top of my head. "Not much. It's him, but he's like an innocent five year old who has no idea what's going on around him. And I didn't see any of those dark images he sent into my head before. I didn't pick up anything that might be taken as evil."

"Good," says Mom.

"But..." says Ryan.

Sebastien's eyes widen. "Yes?"

"Someone's been in his mind."

My best friend Roxanne furrows her brow as she pulls another slice of pizza from the pan that sits on the red-and-white checkered tablecloth. "Someone powerful contacted your father?"

I swallow a bite of the steaming double supreme and wash it down with a sip of my super-sized-anti-Mayor-Bloomberg Dr. Pepper. It's funny, even though the guy's out of office people still associate him with declaring DEFCON ONE on soda, and the pizza parlor actually named its extra large drink the Bloomberg Special when the law got tossed by the courts. It's the New York carbonated middle finger at the guy. The restaurant is crowded for a Sunday night, the Mom-and-Pop eatery filled with loud conversation, the smell of baking pies and the sounds of Sinatra. "That's what Sebastien said. It has to be someone strong to get through their security."

"No way to identify the person?"

I shake my head. "Nope. Not yet, anyway. All Ryan got from my father was that he'd had a visitor."

"So what was this person of power looking for?"

"The theory is that it's one of my father's minions who wanted to determine if his powers are totally fried. Or maybe try to bring him back to full strength. Which scares the hell out of me."

"Aren't you glad you didn't heal him."

"Yeah, no kidding." My heartbeat is picking up a bit and I realize we need to get off the subject. After saving a life on Friday and spending all day at The Summit yesterday, I need something mindless. "So did you and Jake have a good time last night?"

Roxanne surprises me as she shrugs. "Not really. We went to dinner and after that I wanted to go home."

"What happened? I thought he was taking you dancing at that new club?"

"I wasn't in the mood after hearing about his hot Political Science teacher for an hour."

"Hot teacher?"

She rolls her eyes and pushes her shoulder length black hair behind her ears with her hands. "Oooooh, Ms. Cruise. She's soooo interesting and she makes her lectures come alive with her incredibly expressive face and all the boys have a thing for her and it's amazing that she's forty and never married... I mean, I know college boys have it bad for women who are a little older, but geez, it was like he was talking to another guy. Then he goes on and on about a meeting he had with her after class and how she really takes a personal interest in her students and seems to think he's got a future in politics. Finally I'd had enough so I told him I didn't feel well and he took me home."

"Rox, I wouldn't worry about it. Freshmen boys are like kids in a candy store when they see college women after four years of high school girls. Even Ryan's got his head on a swivel."

"Yeah, but *we're* college women now."

"Yeah, but we're eighteen and a forty year old has been around the block already. It's the experience factor, and, as you know, we don't have any." I reach across the table and pat her hand. "Look, you've got nothing to worry about. Besides, if by some strange turn of events things didn't work out with you and Jake there'd be a line of hot guys waiting for a shot at a six foot babe with legs up to her neck. It's not a bad lookin' crop on that campus."

"I suppose. Still, I've got it bad for the little guy and it kinda hurt me a little, ya know?"

"Aren't you the one who always said men take longer to grow up?"

"Stop hitting me with my own logic, short stuff."

"Maybe you need a little of your own logic. Remember when you first started dating him you went out with someone else to keep him in line?"

"I'm not playing those games anymore."

"I'm not saying you should actually do it. But just talk about a male teacher and give him a taste of his own medicine."

"The only male teacher we've got is that eighty year old English professor who died and didn't get the memo."

"Okay, not my best idea. Tell you what, I'll send my alter ego into that classroom and see what the hell is going on with that teacher."

After four years of challenging my stomach to a daily culinary smackdown in a high school cafeteria that served dishes which looked suspiciously like lab experiments, there was no way I was gonna eat college food. Roxanne and I had already done reconnaissance during our spring campus visit and were treated to a mystery meat dish she referred to as "cold shoulder" since a: it was cold, and b: she found a bone in it that looked like a shoulder blade she'd seen in her cousin's butcher shop. Besides, with the campus in Manhattan I could throw a stone and hit any number of terrific and reasonably priced places to eat. However, the school does have a subsidized coffee bar, which offers terrific flavored joes at a dollar a cup, so I'm enjoying a mug of almond amaretto while I attempt to navigate through the 1800s literary version of the health care law, Moby Dick. Get this: the book is required reading for my *Modern Literature* course. Which begs the question, would you have to be living during the Abe Lincoln administration to consider this book *modern*? Anyway, after thirty pages on the care and feeding of whales I'm ready to impale myself on a harpoon and making a point to hit the college bookstore on the way home to pick up the Cliff Notes. Hey, I can spend fifty hours reading this dated monstrosity or getting the thirty minute recap and spending my time doing noble deeds. Seems like a no-brainer to me. I could even do a testimonial for the Cliff Notes people that they could put on the back cover:

> *"The condensed version of Moby Dick gave me the time I needed to save the planet."*
> *-Jillian Spectre, superheroine*

Anyway, the java bar is packed and I'm sitting alone at a corner table for two when a tight pair of jeans moves into my field of vision. I look up and see a Greek god standing before me with a cup of coffee.

"Mind if I join you? All the other seats are taken."

A quick glance around the room tells me this is true. Not that I care with a guy like this, since one does not often encounter mythological figures who look like fashion models, so I gesture toward the chair opposite me. "Sure."

"Thanks." He places his books and coffee on the table as he sits down and slides his chair closer to the table, then extends his hand. "Trip Logan."

My hand looks tiny and disappears into his as we shake. "Jillian Spectre."

His handshake is gentle despite his size. He cocks his head toward my novel. "You're not actually reading that mind-numbing thing, are you?"

I close the book and slide it off to the side. "I made a valiant attempt, but I started to lose interest at *Call me Ishmael*."

"Ah, yes, I remember this school's concept of Modern Literature. When I took it we were reading the Rosetta Stone."

I laugh and take in this vision as he sips his coffee. The guy's built like a linebacker: incredibly broad shoulders, huge ripped biceps straining to escape from his short sleeved shirt, forearms with bulging veins that belong on a blacksmith. One of those men whose chest looks twice as wide as his waist. He obviously lives in the gym. At least six-foot-four, maybe taller. He looks like he could bench press a Toyota but has a silky smooth voice. Throw in the angles-and-planes face, thick black hair, dark brown eyes and dimples, and my heart is beginning to flutter. I think back to Ryan's favorite phrase when he sees a beautiful woman. *"I'm your boyfriend, but I'm not dead."*

I'm not dead either. Besides, with Roxanne's news that Jake has a bit of a wandering eye, I could just be on a scouting mission for her, seeking out young men built like Thor.

Yeah, let's go with that.

I look at his stack of books, a collection of history and political science. "Let me guess... pre-law?"

He nods. "You're very perceptive. I start applying in a couple of months."

"Oh, so you're a senior."

"Yep."

"What kind of law do you want to practice?"

"Criminal. I'd love to be a prosecutor, put bad guys away."

"Very noble. So, not going for the big bucks?"

"Maybe someday, but right now I just want to make the world a better place."

"Yeah, I know the feeling."

He locks his spectacular deep-set eyes with me and it's all I can do to remind myself I'm taken. "I realize that's kind of a naive rose colored glasses way to look at things, but it feels good to help people. So, what do you wanna do?"

"Same deal. Help people. You might say it's in my blood. But right now I don't have a major." I sip my coffee and then it hits me. He's taking political science. "Hey, you ever have a teacher named Ms. Cruise?"

"The Cruise Missile? Nah, I had someone else for freshman poly sci. But I know who she is. Anyway, she apparently knows her subject matter. Served a couple of terms in Congress. She was known for sleeping around there, too."

"What do you mean... *too*?"

"She, uh... well, she has quite the reputation around here. Let's just say it's possible for male students to get extra credit, if you get my drift."

"They call her the Cruise Missile?"

"Legend has it that she zeroes in on one student every semester like a heat seeking missile. Apparently her affairs with freshmen are legendary around here."

"So why is she still teaching here?"

"Because legend has it she also had an affair with the college president, and she's holding that little bit of information over his head. Along with some incriminating photos."

"Wow. I guess I'm not in high school anymore."

"Nope. Welcome to the real world."

Ten minutes worth of great conversation later, he looks at his watch. "Well, off to class." He stands up, slugs down the rest of his coffee and tosses the empty cup in a nearby trash can. "It was nice meeting you, Jillian."

"You too, Trip. See you around the campus."

He grabs his books. "So, uh... would it be too forward of me to ask for your phone number?"

"It wouldn't, if I didn't have a boyfriend."

He playfully puts out his lower lip in a pout. "Figures. The good ones are always taken. Well, see you later."

"Yeah," I say, as he turns and heads out of the room, leaving in his wake a sea of longing looks from every girl in the place.

Including me.

The aforementioned "hot teacher" Rebecca Cruise holds court in a classroom that looks like an amphitheater and has what is commonly known as stadium seating, with the rows sloped downward toward the teacher. I've been in the room for another class, so it's easy to focus on it as I stretch out on the couch. I'm going to materialize in the back row during Jake's class so I can make a quick, unnoticed arrival and getaway.

What I don't expect is to arrive in the dark.

The only light in the room is provided by a projector which is filling the front wall with a PowerPoint presentation while the teacher strolls by the front row.

She comes as advertised.

Ms. Cruise is a tall, stunning, blue-eyed blonde, maybe five-nine with a short leather skirt showing off spectacular legs atop red four inch heels and a tight gathered burgundy top that leaves little to the imagination. Not exactly the *costume de riguer* for a college professor, as she looks more like a middle-aged party girl in search of a red plastic cup. If you looked up "cougar" in the dictionary, you'd see her photo. A quick look around the room shows the class is comprised mostly of guys, all of whom are riveted as she prances around the room. I spot Jake in the front row, the glow from the projection lighting up his face and the fact that he's practically drooling over his teacher as he leans forward on the desk.

Luckily in the last row it's pitch dark, so I'm unnoticed. Besides, no one's sitting back here anyway, as most of the class is crammed into the front half of the room.

Anyway, she's whipping through slides that are highlighting some of the more notable revolutionaries in history, many of whom are guests of the state. (Fuzzball's cute little term for "prisoners.")

"Political resistance has always been the instrument of change throughout history," she says. "It is necessary for societal growth. It's up to each of you to carry the torch and challenge authority.

And you don't need a degree to do that, you can start now. Use your freedom of speech." She launches into this wild monologue which tells me she's a stereotypical radical professor whose main objective is not to teach but to influence her students with her own views.

Then, she says something that makes me sit bolt upright.

"It's a shame that the Spectre phone crashed, because it was on the way to changing society for the better."

My eyes narrow as she extols the virtues of my father, his failed invention, and how it would have allowed people to live in the present and not place any trust in blind faith. I look around the room and see heads nodding in agreement.

Including Jake's.

Which makes no sense. Jake knows how evil my father was. I mean, the guy tried to kill Roxanne, the supposed love of Jake's life. Jake hates him with a passion.

But right now he's smiling, agreeing with the lunatic stuff his teacher is spouting.

So what is this woman doing to him and every other student in this class? And how the hell is she doing it?

This is more than a guy being all gaga over a hot woman. This is something else.

Is she a minion of my father? Is it possible she's got some mind controlling powers? If she's got powers, Sebastien will know.

Finally, after this five minute manifesto about how to possibly recapture the false utopia promised by the Spectre phone, I've had enough.

"Excuse me, I'm just curious," I yell, stopping her in her tracks.

She shades her eyes with her palm as she moves away from the projector, squinting in vain to see who's interrupted her from the back of the room. I know there's no way she can see me in the dark. "Yes?"

"Well, you know, I pay forty grand in tuition in order to learn about political science, not to listen to your opinions. Would it be possible for you to stick to the curriculum and leave your personal views at home?"

A collective "whoa" floats through the room from the students. The teacher's face tightens, her eyes narrow into a glare. "*Excuse* me?"

"Hey, you said we should challenge authority. So I'm challenging yours by saying the Spectre phone was part of the biggest con job in the history of this country. I'm happy it crashed. It would have destroyed society."

"Who's back there? Lights!"

And just before a student in the front row reaches the light switch, I book on outta there.

Chapter 2

I guess I should catch you up on how my powers work these days, since I spent most of the summer working on my newfound projection and healing abilities.

As far as my duties as a seer go, not much has changed. I can still only see five years into the future, still only read romance, still get occasional views of the afterlife. Luckily I'm still in contact with the angel Carrielle, though he hasn't needed me for any special projects since we put my father into a deep freeze. I simply meet him when I need inspiration or advice.

But when it comes to projecting myself to a different location (Ryan refers to my alter ego as Jillian 2.0) I've made significant progress with the help of Fuzzball. My alter ego trips fall into two categories. If I simply project and don't have to heal anyone, I return to my body and wake up immediately feeling perfectly normal. If I have to heal someone during an out of body experience, I need recovery time but I don't black out unless it's a life or death situation, which I have just learned. It's taken less time as I've gotten more experienced, but the rule of thumb is this: the more drastic the healing process, the longer the recovery time. However, I had never saved anyone as close to death as the detective's partner.

Sadly, for Ryan anyway, I cannot be awake in both my real body and the projection at the same time, denying him his fantasy of being with two Jillians at the same time. What is it about men and twins?

Now that school has started, my mystic seer duties are down to two nights a week. Fortunately Fuzzball has helped me replace that lost income by helping him on a few of his moonlighting jobs that all cops seem to have. We're quite the buddy cop duo, projecting ourselves to solve mysteries, which pays pretty well. I'm working for him Friday night, on an assignment that should be a hoot. Politician's wife thinks he's cheating (yeah, there's a real stretch) and she wants to find out if the guy's hot female "consultant" is taking care of more than focus groups.

But right now I've got a new client to take care of, and hopefully I'll be done quick since the Giants are on Monday Night Football and I never miss a game. He's a young guy, probably my age, which is surprising. As you can imagine, most of our clients are older, and most are women. Most college age men aren't exactly worried about romance as they are about sex. (There should be a freshman class to teach them the difference.)

Anyway, this guy has that lost puppy dog look which tells me he's got it bad for some girl. He tells me his name is Stan as he shakes my hand, then sits down opposite me. He's very average looking, five on a scale of one to ten, maybe five-foot-six with a scruffy blonde beard and curly hair to match. He might qualify as a six if he bought a razor.

"So, you have some concerns about romance," I say.

He nods. "There's someone I'm very interested in. And to be perfectly honest, I think she's probably way out of my league."

"Why do you say that?"

"She's really pretty, and I know a lot of guys are interested in her."

"Well, that's true of most attractive women. Doesn't mean you don't have a shot. You might be her type."

"I doubt it. But I'd like to save myself the pain of getting shot down if possible."

"I hear ya. Did you bring a photo?"

"Sorry, don't have one." He describes her, and I can tell he's right about the out-of-his-league thing since she sounds like a supermodel.

"Okay, Stan, here's how this works. I want you to ask a question about romance, and only about romance. Then focus on the question and nothing else. Got it?"

"Sounds simple enough."

"So what's your question?"

"Is it possible for me to have a relationship with her?"

"Now close your eyes and focus."

I do the same and try my best to create a mental picture from the description he's given me, adding his image in the process. I open my eyes and the crystal ball is already fogged up. "Okay, Stan, you can open your eyes."

He looks at the ball and sees the fog. "Wow, that was fast. You see anything?"

"Not yet, but the picture is clearing. It won't take long." The fog dissipates and I see Stan walking along a hallway with a lot of doors. It looks like a bunch of offices. He heads for the door at the end of the hallway and is about to reach for the doorknob when he appears to hear something. He leans his head against the door and listens. The image dissolves to the inside of the office. I can see shadows on the floor, two people kissing. And then I see the two people creating the shadows.

Ms. Cruise.

And Jake.

"She could be a dream weaver."

Mom's words make me furrow my brow. "A what?"

"Dream weaver. It's legend really, as there's no evidence on record that one has ever existed. But it's an old tale about a woman who can manipulate others into thinking they're dreaming when they're actually awake." Mom puts down her coffee, gets up from the kitchen table and heads upstairs. She quickly returns with a very old leather bound book and slides it onto the table. The cover is plain, with no title visible on it or the spine.

"What's this?" I ask.

"Call it the big book of paranormal legends." She flips it open. I see her name, Zelda Spectre, written on the inside cover.

"How old is this thing?"

"I think it was put together around 1900. You're in it, by the way."

My eyes widen. "Excuse me?"

"Remember you were told there was a legend of a seer who could see beyond the physical world?" She flips through the book, stops at a page, turns it around and shoves it in my direction. "There you are."

To say my jaw dropped would be putting it mildly. There I was, a crude pencil drawing like the kind you see in dictionaries. But it was definitely me, complete with freckles. I quickly scan the description of the legendary seer, which describes me perfectly. "When were you gonna show me this?"

She shrugs. "I actually forgot it was in there."

"Your daughter is in a hundred year old book about paranormal legends and you *forgot*?"

"Hey, I'm middle aged. I'm getting C-R-S."

"What's C-R-S?"

"Can't remember shit." She grabs the book and turns it around, then starts flipping through the pages. "Car keys, grocery lists, where my glasses are even though they're on top of my head, lately I can't remember a damn thing. Anyway, I remember reading about the dream weaver when I was a little girl." She stops and points to the middle of a page. "Here it is."

She starts to read aloud but I grab the book.

DREAM WEAVER

A person of high intelligence who is able to manipulate the reality of those around her. Subjects will assume they are having lucid dreams when in reality they are awake. The Dream Weaver is then able to manipulate them into doing anything since the subjects believe they are dreaming and there are no consequences. There is also a mind control factor, as the dream weaver is able to implant thoughts and ideas into the subject. The legend of the Dream Weaver originated in Roman times, when it was said that a general had the ability to make opposing troops march off cliffs while making his own troops lose their fear of death.

There is no evidence to support the existence of a Dream Weaver.

I slide the book back to my mother. "Well, she's a college professor, so that takes care of the high intelligence part."

"A degree doesn't make someone smart, sweetie."

"Good point. Look who's in Congress."

"Tell me more about what you saw in the reading. Jake and this teacher, Miss Whatshername."

"Cruise. Rebecca Cruise. Well, they were in her office at the college. She basically had him pinned against the wall and was kissing him and about to do God knows what else. And she was totally in charge of the situation."

"Was he resisting at all?"

I shake my head. "No, he looked like he was really enjoying it. She started to unbutton his shirt and that's when I ended the reading. I didn't want to see anything else."

"And this teacher, Cruise, she's a supporter of your father?"

"Yeah, big time. You shoulda heard her, building him up like he was some sort of messiah and everyone in the class just eating it up. So the fact that Jake likes her makes no sense."

"Hmmm. If she is a dream weaver she could be manipulating Jake."

"Is there any other paranormal power that would account for something like this?"

She shakes her head. "Don't think so. I'll ask Sebastien but I've read this book cover to cover and there's nothing else that could explain it."

"You think the legend is real, Mom?"

"Hey, the legend about you turned out to be true." She looks at the page. "Too bad there's no illustration of the dream weaver in the book."

"Mom, there's one other thing. I met another student who said this teacher is well known for having affairs with a different freshman every year. You think what I saw means that she's going after Jake?"

"It would make sense. And if she has that kind of power, she could also be the one who made contact with your father."

Roxanne slowly picks at her Monterrey Jack chicken, head down, not remotely herself as we have a casual dinner on this Friday night. No, I haven't told her what I saw in the reading or about the possibility of a dream weaver doing a Manchurian Candidate thing on Jake and turning him into her own personal boy-toy. It would push her over the edge. I'm hoping our double date of dinner, a movie and dancing will cheer her up. The restaurant is one of those casual fun chains, where all the waiters and waitresses bounce around like they've had a six pack of Red Bull and you can win a fried cheese appetizer if you answer the trivia question of the night.

Ryan's been briefed and sworn to secrecy. His mission tonight: to take a quiet trip into Jake's mind during the movie and find out what the hell the Cruise Missile has done to him. Sebastien is coming by tomorrow to get a full report. Meanwhile, he has no information at all on Ms. Cruise. If she has powers, she's totally off the grid. And Mom was right, there's no other paranormal power that could account for what's happening.

Jake is his usual talkative self, totally oblivious to the fact Roxanne looks very depressed. He hasn't said anything about the teacher in question, but something is different about him. Can't put my finger on it, but I'll figure it out.

"Rox, your food okay?" I ask.

She shrugs and gives me a sad look. "Yeah, it's fine."

"Is it just me," I say, going on our pre-planned fishing expedition, "or are freshman college courses beyond boring?"

"Tell me about it," says Ryan. "I've got a couple of professors who I think died in 2010 and no one's told them. But I guess we've gotta get the required courses out of the way. I sure hope it gets better, because four years of this would be torture."

"I dunno, I've got a couple of good courses," says Jake. Roxanne glares at me, as if to say *why the hell did you bring this up*? "I like a couple of my classes."

Ryan pops a French fry and talks through it. "You got that whack job radical political science professor, right?"

"Who, Ms. Cruise? She seems pretty conservative to me."

And now I know the woman has some power.

Chapter 3

I'm deep in thought as I wait for the crosswalk light to change to the little green man. And I have to admit I'm frustrated. My first weeks of college were supposed to be fun, meeting people who actually have ambition as opposed to the human doorstops who made up half of our student body. Of course, this being a very expensive school (thank goodness we all have full scholarships), there are a few girls working on a MRS degree with a trust fund brat, of which there are many. Overall, the whole college experience has been extremely disappointing, and when you throw in the fact I'm still doing my superheroine thing while dealing with a possible dream weaver who might be trying to access my father, I'm ready for spring break in September.

And after another Saturday with Sebastien there are more questions than answers. The geek squad at The Summit has tried everything in the book but can't get a read on the Cruise Missile. However, they're convinced she does have some sort of mind control powers. She may not be the legendary dream weaver, but she's a snake oil salesgirl who is selling stuff that is hazardous to your health and could necessitate a penicillin shot for one lucky male freshman. Meanwhile, what she's done to Jake has me worried and Roxanne upset. He's noticeably changed. Nothing major, but he's not the same and it's playing havoc with their relationship.

Sebastien has a theory that those under my father's domain know the four of us took him down and are working on some plan to split us apart. To me that makes perfect sense. After all, we were pretty unbeatable when we combined our powers. Divide and conquer is an old but effective strategy.

The crosswalk light changes and I'm still trying to sort all this out, so I'm not paying attention as I step off the curb right into a hole and twist my ankle. Pain shoots up my leg as I crouch down—

"Look out!"

I look up and see a taxi barreling straight for me, obviously ignoring the red light. My heart rate skyrockets but an arm wraps around my waist and lifts me out of harm's way in the nick of time. The cab flies through the intersection, colliding with a city bus.

"You okay?" asks the voice attached to the arm still holding me in midair.

"Yeah. God, thank you." My heart is still pounding as I'm returned to the ground, which causes a shooting pain in my ankle. "Owww!" The arm steadies me and I lean on it, then turn around to find out the identity of my white knight.

"Oh, it's you," says Trip. "Jillian, right?"

"Yeah. Trip, I don't know what to say. You saved my life."

"Eh, you probably would've rolled out of the way."

"Doubtful."

"You need to pay attention when you cross the street in New York, young lady. A red light doesn't necessarily mean traffic stops."

"Yes, Sir, I'll be a good little girl and look both ways in the future."

He looks down at my leg. "Did you twist your ankle?"

"Yeah, I stepped in that pothole and must have sprained it. Hurts like hell." I try to put some weight on it again but the pain makes me wince.

He wraps one arm around my back to steady me. "I think we need to get you to the school infirmary."

"You're probably right. At least get some ice on it." I stick my hand straight out into the street.

"What are you doing?"

"Hailing a cab. I can't walk on this."

"Don't be ridiculous." Trip reaches down, wraps his other arm under my legs and easily lifts me, cradling my body as he starts walking in the direction of the campus.

"What are you doing?"

"It's only two blocks, and I'm cheaper than a taxi."

"You think you can carry me that far?"

"I dunno, you weigh a ton."

"Hey!" I playfully slap his arm.

He shoots me a grin, one of those sly smiles that makes your heart (and other parts of your body) do somersaults. What the hell, I guess I can be a damsel in distress and get rescued by a handsome block of granite. I relax and wrap my arms around his neck to hold on, feeling his rock-hard muscles under his shirt. He effortlessly carries me down the street. We get to the crosswalk and have to wait for the light. He looks at me and smiles again.

And I'm the one breathing heavy.

I hate to say this, being Ryan's girl and all, but I'm feeling some serious electricity.

This "I'm not dead" thing has some dangerous aspects to it.

My ankle is completely healed after two full days off my feet. Being able to send my alter ego to class was a real asset, so I didn't miss a thing while getting well. However, at one point my projection fell asleep in Economics class and for a moment I ended up back at home. Good thing I'm now a back row girl.

So I'm enjoying the school's welcome-to-the-outside-world dance on this Friday night with Ryan, Roxanne and Jake. Most of the students are freshmen wanting to take advantage of this educationally approved meat market. But there are plenty of upperclassmen as well, ready to swoop in on what Roxanne refers to as "starry-eyed freshmen" girls. College is, as Mom said, a sexual candy store, and everyone has a pocketful of change.

Apparently the school's idea of decorating for a dance is to dim the lights, as the large, rectangular meeting room looks like... wait for it... a large, rectangular meeting room with dim lights. The guys are currently being checked out by one of the school chaperones, the aforementioned Ms. Cruise, who has been licking her lips and giving seductive looks to anything in pants. She's in another cougar outfit, short skirt and tight top, and I note the other teachers are keeping their distance though the males of the species can't stop staring. I've seen Jake looking in her direction a few times, though he hasn't mentioned her and has been paying attention to Roxanne. (We still haven't told him we suspect someone's playing games with his mind, though that may change shortly.) Rox understands there's something going on in the thought control department and is being a real team player by not reading him the riot act.

"Ladies room?" I ask her.

She takes a quick look at Ms. Cruise, who is looking at our table like a cat eyes a canary. "Think I'd better keep an eye on things. Let's tag team. You go first."

I nod. "Sure. Be right back."

I get up and head toward the hall leading to the restroom, then notice there's a giant octopus playing keyboard for the band. I stop dead in my tracks and look around, then see George Washington on the dance floor, doing the jitterbug with Hillary Clinton.

I'm dreaming.

This one's incredibly lucid, so I wonder if Carrielle is hanging out here somewhere. Maybe he has some news about the dream weaver.

"Jillian."

I hear a voice coming from outside the hall. It's not Carrielle, and I don't recognize it, but I decide to follow it, passing a ten-foot blue lobster carrying a tray of champagne glasses who says hello. I move out of the room and into a dimly lit hallway.

"Jillian."

"Who's there?"

No answer.

I keep heading down the hallway. The music fades behind me, until I can't hear it any longer and my heel clicks on the linoleum provide the only sound. I see a silhouette of a man leaning against the wall. He stands up straight and suddenly a soft ethereal light emanates from his body, making him look like an angel.

It's Trip Logan.

"Hey, it's my lifesaver," I say, stopping in front of him. "What are you doing here?"

"It's your dream. You tell me."

"I'm not sure. I didn't even know I was dreaming until a minute ago."

"Maybe you've been thinking about me since I saved your life."

"That explains it."

"Or maybe you've been thinking about me for other reasons."

"Well, you did ask for my phone number. And I am unattached."

Something seems odd as I say that, but I can't put my finger on it. What the hell, it's a dream and a serious hunk is glowing and obviously interested in me.

He moves closer, near enough that I can smell his earthy cologne. Trip is about a foot taller, so his chest is at eye level. He reaches toward me and gently runs his fingers through my hair. He lifts my chin with one finger, locks eyes with me, and suddenly the world disappears. His look is almost hypnotic, and I'm powerless to turn away. Not that I want to. I feel myself being drawn in, like I'm going into a trance. "So, Jillian, you figured out why I'm here?"

"I *have* been thinking about you. The way you saved me. I loved how it felt when you carried me." I slide my hands up along his arms, stopping on his biceps for a brief visit before ending up on his shoulders. "I felt so safe, so protected." I reach my arms up around his neck.

He bends down and lifts me by my hips. I wrap my legs around his waist, grab his head with my hands and our lips meet with a hunger I've never experienced. The ethereal light grows stronger, emanating from me as well, seeming to gain strength from our passion.

"Jillian!"

Someone's calling me but I don't care. It's my dream and this is too damn good. I keep kissing Trip, running my hands along his massive shoulders, then inside his shirt onto his toned chest.

"Jillian! What the hell?"

Oh, for goodness sake, what? I break the liplock and look to the side.

Ryan.

The ride home is excruciating. Ryan's jaw and fists have been clenched the whole time. I've been looking at the floor of the subway car. Luckily we're the only people in it, so we can talk. Not that we've been doing much of that.

Right now I'm dead sure I'm not dreaming.

And never was.

But it seemed so dreamlike. The famous people, the lobster and octopus. The glow from Trip's body. The fact that I didn't think twice about jumping into the arms of Trip Logan, something I would never do in real life. And that I told him I was unattached.

Because I couldn't remember I have a boyfriend who I love very much.

Then, it was like the alarm clock went off when I heard Ryan's voice. I was jolted back into reality and got walloped with a massive dose of guilt.

Ryan was furious, ready to blow. If he were a cartoon character, steam would have come out of his ears. I dropped out of Trip's arms and put my body between them, hoping they wouldn't get into some sort of duel over me. I mean, my boyfriend is well-built but Trip probably has sixty or seventy pounds on him and looks as though he could easily break Ryan in half.

Trip did the honorable thing and managed to diffuse the

situation with some quick thinking, telling Ryan he didn't know I was taken and he'd had too much to drink. He apologized, beat a hasty retreat and left us alone.

Still, what was *my* excuse? My words sounded incredibly lame. I mean, think about it, you tell the guy you love, "Sorry, I thought I was dreaming so I was giving a tonsillectomy to a guy who is off the charts gorgeous while it looked like he was going to carry me off to the bedroom."

I even told him to read my mind, and he did, but for some reason it didn't back up my story. What I remembered was *not* what Ryan picked up, as he never saw the dream characters. All he saw was his girlfriend acting like a cheap slut about to hook up with another guy. Why I can remember it and he can't read it is something we need to figure out, and fast.

I'm biting my lip, trying to hold back tears as he stares straight ahead at a Broadway show poster for *Wicked* that hangs on the opposite wall of the subway car. The only sound is the train rumbling over the tracks. I slide my hand over, putting it on top of his, and his face relaxes a bit. "I hope you know I love you, Ryan."

He doesn't say anything, but slowly nods.

Progress.

"Something is happening to us. To me and Jake. Something we cannot control. I don't know what it is but I'm going to find out."

"Yeah," he says, barely audible. He turns to me, eyes wet. "Jillian, if it was a dream, why would you have been thinking of him?"

He doesn't trust me. He never calls me Jillian. I'm always Sparks.

"Remember the guy who pulled me out of the street the other day? It was him. He's really a nice guy—"

His eyes narrow into a glare.

"Sorry."

"Are you attracted to him?"

"I'm in love with *you*."

"You didn't answer the question."

"I believe I just did, Ryan." I squeeze his hand.

He goes back to staring at the poster, and I wonder if he now thinks of me as the Wicked Witch of the West. I know it's gonna be a while before he can get the image of me and Trip that's burned into his brain out of his head.

Problem is, it's burned into my brain too.

Chapter 4

Mom is already reading the New York tabloids with her morning coffee as I trudge down the stairs. She looks into my bloodshot, puffy eyes and her face tells me she instantly knows something is very wrong. "Jillian, what happened?"

I move across the kitchen, pour a cup of coffee and sit down across from her. "I think the dream weaver got me last night, Mom."

She sits up straight. "What?"

"It's a long story, and it wasn't my fault... but I sorta cheated on Ryan."

Her eyes widen as I tell her the story, from meeting Trip Logan to him saving my life to the dance. And the fact that Ms. Cruise was in the building and obviously got into my head.

"So this Trip fellow... that was the guy who pulled you out of the traffic the other day?"

I nod.

"And you were absolutely sure you were dreaming?"

"I was convinced, Mom. I saw things that couldn't possibly be real. I never would have cheated on Ryan. But when I ran into Trip, I couldn't even remember that I had a boyfriend. I told him I was unattached."

"Hmmm. The dream weaver has obviously gotten into your subconscious. Are you attracted to this guy?"

"He's beyond good looking, Mom, but I love Ryan."

"Not what I asked, Missy. Do you find him attractive?"

"Well, yeah. Sure. I think you'd be hard pressed to find a woman who *didn't* think he was attractive. Physically he's off the charts, and he's nice, too. I have to admit I was flattered that he asked for my phone number when we first met because guys like that can hook up with supermodels."

"She obviously tapped into that and used him to tempt you. I think Sebastien was right, they're trying to come between the four of you."

"Makes sense." I stare into my coffee cup. "Mom, there's something else."

"What?"

"Well, I don't know how to put this... but when I was kissing Trip in the dream, or what I thought was a dream, well, I felt something. A real connection that I don't feel with Ryan."

"You weren't yourself, sweetie. Hey, if I had a dream and ran into Bradley Cooper I'd rip his clothes off."

"You got a thing for Bradley Cooper?"

"I'm middle-aged, honey, I'm not dead. Anyway, you're being manipulated."

"God, I hope that's it."

She reaches across the table and takes my hands. "Let me tell you something about love. It's not about finding someone you can live with, but finding someone you can't live without."

Once again, parents can sometimes simplify things. It makes perfect sense.

"Could you live without Ryan?"

"No way, Mom."

I decide to do a little damage control and stop by Ryan's dorm room with a small peace offering. Even though Mom says I've done nothing wrong and it wasn't my fault, I know I've hurt him. The kind of hurt that doesn't go away quickly, and I know how fragile a guy's ego can be, even a self-confident guy like Ryan. I've got a box of red velvet cupcakes, his favorite, from Roxanne's family bakery. Just as I'm about to knock on the door he comes up behind me, dripping with sweat, carrying a gym bag.

"Hey, Sparks, good timing."

He didn't call me Jillian. Maybe he's not mad anymore.

I lean forward and give him a quick kiss. "Brought you a present." I hand him the box and he smiles as he sees it's from the bakery.

"Thanks. You didn't have to do this. I'm okay."

"I don't need a reason to do nice things for the man I love. So, you and Jake been playing racquetball?"

"We're playing later today. I joined the campus health club. It's free to students and you get a personal trainer for your first visit."

I scrunch up my face. "Isn't racquetball enough exercise for one day? Since when are you a gym rat?"

He opens the door to the room, holds it for me and I walk inside. "Racquetball is a great workout, but I wanna get strong. I started lifting weights. Trainer says I could add ten pounds of muscle since I'm only one-seventy. I started boxing classes as well."

Oh, crap. I know what this is about. When it comes to men everything boils down to that "size matters" bullshit. He saw me with a guy who's a lot taller and bigger than him and built like a comic book superhero. "I don't suppose this has anything to do with what happened the other night."

"I just thought it was time to tone up. You know. Get buffed. For you."

"Uh-huh." He moves inside and I close the door behind him. He puts his gym bag away, grabs a towel, and wipes his face. "Ryan, look at me."

He turns to face me. "What?"

I move forward and take his arms. "You don't have to change a thing for me. You're perfect the way you are."

"You're only saying that because you love me."

I shake my head and exhale in frustration. "Does the stupidity of what you just said even register in that head of yours?"

"What? It's true. You don't want to hurt my feelings because you love me."

I look to the side and do my anchorwoman voice. "Let's recap that last idiotic statement for those of you who just tuned in." I turn back to him and tap him on the head with a knuckle. "Hello! McFly! What were those last three words you said? Huh?"

"You love me."

"Now, would you like to go for *Double Jeopardy* where the scores can really change? Maybe if you focus on those three words you'll realize I say things to you because they're true. *Because* I love you. So yes, you're perfect for me. I thought of you that way before we started dating. You're a six-foot hunk without an ounce of fat, and I oughta know because I've conducted a thorough search. You don't have to get all musclebound because I'm already yours and you have a hammerlock on my heart that no one is going to break."

"I wanna be strong for you. Be able to protect you."

Damn. Guys just don't get it.

I snake my arms around his neck and give him a soulful look. "Ryan, there's more to being strong than just physical strength, which, I might add, you already have. You've been my emotional rock since I've known you. I never had a father and you *always* protected me and took care of me, even when we were little. I've always been able to lean on you. And, in case you've forgotten, you almost gave your life to save me a few months ago. Which was the second time you nearly died for me. I couldn't find a stronger guy than you if I tried."

He grows a hangdog look and his face drops.

"This is about what happened at the dance, isn't it?" I ask.

He nods, still looking at the floor. "I was, you know, feeling a little... inadequate."

I take his chin and lift it so he's facing me. "Stop it. Stop it right now, young man. There's nothing inadequate about you.

Any girl would be thrilled to have you and I'm incredibly lucky to be that girl."

"I just... felt like such a shrimp next to him."

I roll my eyes. "Obviously you're not getting my point. You talk to Jake a lot, right?"

"Yeah."

"And in case you hadn't noticed, he's got an amazon girlfriend who towers over him and yet is madly in love with him. She doesn't think he's a shrimp. Hell, she wears four inch heels around him. She's proud to be seen with him."

"Yeah. I guess."

"You guess? For God's sake, Ryan, I love you! Do I have to have sex with you to prove it?"

"No, of course not. We agreed to wait."

"Good, because you shouldn't need it to know how I feel. What happened the other night wasn't me."

"Deep down I know that, Sparks. But it's still hard to compete with a guy like that."

Roxanne's bite of bagel nearly falls out of her mouth as she looks at Trip sitting down at the opposite end of the coffee bar. "*That's* the guy you made out with?"

I take a look and nod as I sip my coffee. "Yeah. Trip Logan."

"Yowza. Damn, Jillian, at least the dream weaver has good taste. I'm not sure I'd wanna wake up."

"Down, girl. You're still taken, remember?"

"I know, but geez, he looks computer generated. You basically had a fantasy come true and got a *get out of jail free* card."

"Doesn't make me feel any better about it. And I didn't get away free. It really hurt Ryan. He's still upset."

"Hell, I don't blame him. The equivalent would be me seeing Jake making out with a supermodel."

"And get this... Ryan joined the health club. Started weight training and boxing lessons."

Rox shakes her head and rolls her eyes. "If men have one common denominator, you just found out what it is."

I take a quick look at Trip, who is busy reading a book. "That's not the only thing bothering me, Rox." I lower my voice to a whisper. "I... uh... can't stop thinking about it. Me and Trip, I mean. What happened the other night is stuck in my head."

"I wouldn't be able to forget either. But as long as you're just thinking, you won't need to go to confession."

"It's not just that he's incredibly hot. Remember when you went out last year with that football player?"

"The crash test dummy? Yeah, what about it?"

"Remember how you didn't feel anything? Well, this was different. I felt something with Trip I never felt with Ryan."

"That's 'cause you were dreaming. Or thought you were."

I shake my head. "No, no, there was something else. We were, I don't know, it was like we were connected on a different level. There was an electricity about it, like we were meant to be together."

"Jillian, stop it." She stares at Trip over her coffee cup, then turns back to me. "You caught the sexual brass ring for a couple of minutes, that's all. You're acting like a man."

"What do you mean by that?

"You're thinking with the wrong head." She looks at Trip again. "It will pass."

"She says as she stares at the guy and drools all over the table."

"Hey, it doesn't matter where I work up my appetite as long as I have dinner at home."

"I'm sure Jake would appreciate knowing that. Meanwhile, I need to talk to Trip."

Her eyes widen. "Are you out of your mind? You're only gonna make things worse. What if Ryan walks in?"

"He's got class right now. Rox, I need to know what really happened, I need his point of view. What I remember and what Ryan saw when he read my mind are two very different things. I need to know why there are two different memories in my head of the same event. I promise, this will be the last time I ever talk to him."

"I'm tellin' ya, you're playing with fire."

"I'll be fine."

Roxanne finishes her bagel, wipes her mouth with a napkin and stands up. "Okay, but I gotta get to class in five minutes, so I can't keep an eye on you."

"Really, I'll be okay."

"Well, if you're gonna do this at least take me over and introduce me."

"Working up that appetite?"

"I want an up close and personal look at Mister Universe. I'm attached, but I'm not dead."

I get up and lead her over to Trip's table. He's engrossed in his book as we approach. He looks up and his eyes widen and fill with a touch of concern. "Uh... Jillian. Hi. You sure this is a good idea?"

"We need to talk, Trip. Oh, this is my best friend, Roxanne."

He stands up and extends his hand. Rox does all she can to keep her jaw from hanging open as she looks up at him but is unsuccessful. This is one of the few guys who's taller than her in her heels. "Hi, Trip Logan."

She shakes his hand. "Uh-huh."

She doesn't say anything else as he sits down. I give her a gentle elbow in the ribs. "You've got class, right?"

"Whuh?" Her eyes are still locked on him. "Class, right. Nice to meet ya."

"My pleasure," he says. Rox turns and walks right into a chair, nearly falls, then continues out of the coffee bar. I grab a chair opposite Trip and sit down.

"Look, Trip, what happened the other night—"

He puts up his hands. "I promise, it won't happen again. You don't have to worry about me coming between you and your boyfriend. I'll keep my distance."

"It's not that. I wasn't myself and... Well, I need to know what

I said."

"You don't remember?"

"I can't handle my liquor." I've never even had alcohol, but it's the best excuse I can come up with.

"Okay. Well, I went out in the hall to use my cell, and just as I finished the call I saw you, so I shouted out to you."

"I remember that. What happened next?"

"You asked me what I was doing there, which I thought was an odd question. I told you I'd come to the dance."

"You didn't say anything about dreams?"

His brow tightens. "Dreams? What dreams?"

"Not important. So then what did I say?"

"You said you'd been thinking about me, and I said I'd been thinking about you too but it was really frustrating since you had a boyfriend. You started to laugh and I asked you what was so funny. Then you said you were unattached, that you always told guys you just met you had a boyfriend. Until you got to know them better. Just to be safe. And then you said you wanted to get to know me better, that I seemed like a good guy after saving you from getting hit by the cab."

"I said that?"

"Yeah. So now I'm thinking I have a shot with you so I got excited. Jillian, I was very interested from the moment I met you. I hadn't stopped thinking about you."

"Me? I would think a guy who looks like you would have women beating down your door."

He actually blushes a bit. "There's something about you, Jillian. I'm mean, you're gorgeous and all but you have this incredible life force thing going that takes it to another level. Anyway, when you almost got hit by the car and I got to spend a little time with you, it made things worse. I'll admit I got turned on carrying you down the street when you put your arms around me. It was driving me crazy that you had a boyfriend because I desperately wanted a chance with you."

I must say I'm getting really flattered at this point, and now I'm beginning to blush, but I need to stick to the task at hand. "Okay, so what happened next?"

"Well, you started talking about how I saved your life and how you felt protected when I carried you to the infirmary. How you hadn't properly thanked me and wanted to do it in private. You started sliding your hands up my arms, then around my neck and you gave me this look that went right into my soul. Then you jumped into my arms, wrapped your legs around me and started kissing me. Then you asked me to take you back to my place. That's when your boyfriend showed up."

"You didn't make the first move? You didn't pick me up?"

He shakes his head. "No, you took the initiative. And you certainly weren't shy about it."

"And I asked you to take me to your place?"

He nods. "Yeah."

"Were you going to?"

"A guy doesn't pass up an invitation like that from a girl like you. But then your boyfriend showed up. Talk about a disappointing end to an evening." He looks around, leans forward and lowers his voice. "Look, Jillian, I'm sorry you got in trouble with your boyfriend, but I never would have let it happen if you hadn't said you were unattached. I don't want you to think of me as one of those guys who breaks up relationships."

"I don't. And I want to thank you for the way you handled it. That was quick thinking on your part. It would have ended up much worse."

"Well, I understand how he feels, and I'd feel the same way. He obviously cares for you a great deal. Lucky bastard."

"Actually, I'm the lucky one."

"So how are things with your boyfriend? He looked pretty angry."

I shrug. "He's hurt, but he's tough. He'll get over it."

"Good. Not sure I will."

"Excuse me?"

He leans forward and locks eyes with me. "Jillian, I know we were only kissing for a minute or two, but what I felt with you is something I've never felt before."

Jake and I are riding to The Summit on this Saturday morning. Mom's backed up on her clients, so she isn't tagging along. Sebastien only wanted to see the two of us since we're the ones who have been affected. Roxanne and Ryan are patiently waiting at home, both of whom hoping for something that will explain why the people they love suddenly seem interested in others. But them being left behind is fine since I wanted a chance to talk with Jake and bring him into the loop. While I know I've been affected, he doesn't think anything is different.

"Trust me, Jake, you've changed."

"I changed last year, remember? In a good way."

"I know. But you're doing stuff you wouldn't normally do. And I've been meaning to talk to you about it since Roxanne hasn't."

He turns to me as I drive and keep my eyes on the road. "What's up with Rox?"

I exhale deeply, knowing she didn't want me to talk about it, but I can't let this go on. It's hurting her too much. "Jake, you've been talking about another woman when you're out with her."

"No I haven't. I would never do that."

"You've been doing it. You just don't realize it."

"Well, then, who am I talking about?"

"Your teacher, Ms. Cruise."

"That's different, Jillian. I was just talking about a teacher I like, that's all."

"Yeah, but the way it comes out, it sounds like you're interested in her. Romantically."

"That's ridiculous. Cruise is old enough to be my mother. And I love Roxanne."

"I know you do, and she knows you do. But your teacher has

seriously screwed with your mind." I can tell he doesn't believe me, so I decide to tell him about seeing him in a reading. "Okay, you have to pinky swear with me that you will not tell Roxanne what I'm about to tell you."

His face tightens. "What?"

"Pinky swear." I stick out my pinky.

He shakes it with his. "Yeah, sure. So what's the big secret?"

"I saw you in my crystal ball the other night."

"You did a reading for Roxanne?"

"No, Jake. It was a reading for someone else who is a student at our college, but you were in it. You were kissing Ms. Cruise. And it looked like you were going to go a lot further."

We're both propped up on a couple of hospital beds with electrodes attached to our heads. Jake is noticeably upset about what's been going on with Cruise, especially after talking with Sebastien about her. After two hours of testing, I'm ready for answers.

But when Sebastien walks in with a worried look, I know I'm not getting the answers I want.

"You can remove the wires now," he says. Jake and I quickly pull the sticky connectors from our foreheads.

"So, what's the verdict?' I ask.

Sebastien looks down at a printout. "Both of you have been affected in the same way."

"How so?" asks Jake.

"Your brain waves have been altered."

My eyes widen. "Altered?"

"The patterns have changed slightly. In the Delta waves."

"The subconscious ones," says Jake. "The ones her father wanted to access in her."

"Correct," says Sebastien. "Jake, I know you would like to drop this class, but if we are to study this situation we need you to remain close."

"I understand," he says. "Not sure Roxanne will, though."

"And Jillian, I need you to monitor her class, but only using your alter ego. Remember, she cannot access your brain waves when you are a projection. We will need to compare what Jake takes from the class to what she is actually saying."

"Okay. So... what does this mean?" I ask. "Can we be, you know, fixed?"

Sebastien looks at the floor. "I'm told it's like a virus in your brain waves. Right now we have no idea how to deal with it, but at least we have isolated the problems."

"So how do I know when I'm dreaming and when I'm not?" I ask.

He shakes his head. "Unfortunately, I cannot answer that question. You will simply have to be very careful."

"If it's a virus, like the computer virus we gave to Jillian's father, will we get sick?" asks Jake.

"It's not physical, it's mental," says Sebastien. "But when you take that into account with the things you both have been experiencing, it serves to confirm our suspicions."

"And those suspicions would be?" I ask.

"That the dream weaver exists."

It's a beautiful fall day, late in the afternoon, temperatures in the seventies and low humidity. The leaves will be changing soon, the maples bringing color to my favorite month, October, which is just around the corner. It's a perfect day for a walk to clear my head, which currently has all sorts of problems bouncing around like bingo balls. When I shove one concern to the back burner, another moves to the front.

The streets are surprisingly quiet, the only sounds coming from the dribbling of a basketball at a nearby court. I look ahead and see there's only one guy shooting hoops. Maybe I'll join him. I've got a pretty decent jump shot and I could use some exercise.

The guy has his back to me, but he's shirtless and what I can see is impressive. His well-defined shoulder muscles twitch with every shot. Each time the ball swishes through the hoop, nothing but net, and comes right back to him. He starts to dribble a bit, tries a bank shot, misses. The ball rolls toward me and he gives chase as I bend down to pick it up.

When I stand back up I'm face to face with Trip Logan. "Oh, Trip, it's you."

"Hi Jillian." He reaches down to a bench, grabs a towel, and begins to mop his brow. His chiseled body is glistening with sweat. The sight of him in just a pair of shorts makes me gulp. My original assessment of him as a Greek god was correct.

"I was, uh, out for a walk."

He smiles at me as he moves closer and drapes the towel over his neck. "Uh-huh. You know, Jillian, for a girl who needs to avoid me, you sure do seem to run into me a lot."

"Coincidence."

"Coincidences are destiny's favorite trick when it comes to romance."

"I already have someone, Trip. I thought we cleared that up."

He grabs a bottle of water from his gym bag, takes a sip, and puts it on the bench. "I still can't get that night out of my head, Jillian. That feeling hasn't gone away." He reaches out, tilts my chin up, the way he did at the dance. My pulse quickens as his touch brings the now familiar electricity.

"Trip, this isn't a good idea. I... I really should go."

"You don't have to. We're just talking."

"Talking with you is dangerous."

"Why? You afraid it might lead to something that you actually *want* to do?"

"Trip, I really need to go. Being here is not a good idea."

He moves a bit closer, locks eyes with me. "You know you're attracted to me, Jillian. We're meant to be together. Why are you fighting it?"

My heart rate kicks up another notch. "Because I love Ryan."

He nods. "You may *love* Ryan. But you *want* me."

And I know what he says is true.

"You know I do things to you that he doesn't." He gently takes my shoulders and pulls me closer.

His look, his touch, take my breath away and render me powerless. I can't stop myself. My hands come up like they have a mind of their own and rest on his sides, then slide forward as I run them across his washboard abs. The sensation steals my breath and sends fireworks through my heart. "Oh. My. God."

"Problem?"

"Not with your body."

"It's all yours if you want it."

I'm staring at his abs, his chest, hypnotized by the feel of his muscles. It's like nothing I've ever experienced. "Please, Trip. Let me go."

He takes his hands off my shoulders and gives me a casual smile. "Nothing's keeping you here, Jillian. You can leave anytime you want."

My head tells me to leave but my feet seem to be stuck in cement while my hands are busy exploring. They slide up onto his chest, then across his shoulders and around his neck as I look up into his eyes.

"Thought you were leaving."

"I really need to go, Trip."

"So go."

"I... I can't."

He licks his lips as he looks down into my soul. "Do you want something?"

I'm craning my neck as I look up at him. "I do, but... you're awfully tall."

"I could come down there if you like."

"You already know I'm not afraid of heights."

I stretch my arms straight up, like a little girl asking to be picked up. He puts his hands on my sides and effortlessly lifts me up so I'm at eye level. I lean forward to kiss him—

And I jerk bolt upright in bed, heart pounding, my body covered in sweat. My hand goes to my chest as I try to calm down and slow my breathing. I throw back the soaking wet covers, get up, and head to the bathroom to wash my face.

First I couldn't tell reality from a dream. Now I can't tell a dream from reality.

And I have to get Trip Logan out of my head.

I need help, and I know there is only one place to get it.

Chapter 5

"Please come back with some answers," says Roxanne, as I lie down on the couch in the muse office above her family bakery.

"I'll do my best. You know there's no guarantee I'll run into Carrielle."

"Well, the only two people you ever saw when we did this are your father and the angel, and since your father is basically out of commission I think the angel is a good bet."

"Right about that. Okay, let's rock."

Roxanne goes into muse mode as I focus on her eyes. As before, they turn into diamonds as she locks onto my subconscious and the world around us fades.

And dissolves into an outdoor carnival.

I immediately know I'm not going to run into my father, as I see a banner across the midway which reads "Welcome to the 1955 State Fair!"

I find myself walking a midway as buzzers from old fashioned carnival games and the smells of junk food fill the air. Screams ring out in the distance as a roller coaster rumbles by, while a guy in a straw hat implores me to try and win a stuffed animal at his booth.

"Welcome, Jillian."

I turn to see the angel Carrielle behind me. He holds out a

cone of pink cotton candy, my favorite fair food when I was a little girl. My eyes light up and for a moment I'm seven years old again. "I'm so glad you came." I take the cotton candy and inhale a bite. "Oh, yeah. Thank you."

"You have much stress in your life right now," he says, as he walks beside me while eating from a bag of roasted peanuts. He touches my forehead, which is what he does when he gives me peace, and every bit of stress immediately disappears. "I sensed that you needed to relax."

"That's an understatement. But I need your help, Carrielle."

He nods as he leads me to the Ferris wheel and hands the attendant two tickets. We both get into the car, the operator shuts the door, and we take flight. "In case you had any desire to take me on a roller coaster, you should know this is the only ride I can handle," I say. "The fast ones make me sick."

"As I said, you need to relax. This is very peaceful and gives you time to take in nature's glory. It is a particularly beautiful evening."

The car moves forward as it heads up, then backwards as we move to the top of the wheel. It stops there, offering a spectacular view of the ocean at sunset as the sunlight shimmers on the water. "Wow, that's gorgeous."

"One of God's daily gifts. So many do not take the time to appreciate it."

"It is beautiful. But lately I've been wishing I didn't have a certain gift."

"I understand. It is much responsibility for someone as young as yourself. Alas, we are never given more than we can handle. You are stronger than you think, Jillian. You proved that earlier this year. You were chosen to receive these gifts because you have special qualities."

"I'm just an average teenage girl."

He shakes his head and smiles. "You are anything but average."

"Carrielle, I can't think straight. This dream weaver, or whatever you call it, is playing mind games with me."

"Yes, I've been monitoring."

"So what do you know about Rebecca Cruise?"

He looks out toward the ocean. "She has powers, though we cannot read them. Much like your father, dark forces surround her and prevent us from getting information."

"So what's happening to me, Carrielle?"

"You are being tempted, your love for Ryan tested. Your mind is being manipulated in the direction the dark forces want it to go."

"For what purpose? I mean, even if Ryan and I broke up, which isn't going to happen, that's not going to send society into the dumper."

"We can only surmise that she was one of your father's followers, and therefore has a similar objective."

"Speaking of him, do you know who has accessed his mind?"

"Dark forces still control him, though he is powerless. But his mind may contain many secrets, perhaps more of his plan to take down society that he never implemented."

"But his company's gone, the technology failed."

"One does not need technology to topple society. Words are still the most powerful weapons."

"I get it. The pen is mightier than the sword."

"And if this woman is adept at mind control, as she seems to be, then she may be carrying out his original goal in a different way."

The Ferris wheel starts moving again, faster, the breeze blowing through my red tangles as the salt air fills my lungs. We zip through the bottom of the loop and head skyward again. "Carrielle, I'm really confused. I love Ryan but I'm having these feelings about another guy. Feelings I can't explain. And now he's filling my dreams. He's incredibly attractive and I feel somehow drawn to him."

"He is obviously the focal point in the plan. She is throwing the biggest temptation she can find at you, to destroy your love. And, probably, your faith. She may be manipulating his mind as well."

"Well, her plan is working because he's tempting me, all right.

And it makes sense that he's being controlled because he's a guy who could have any woman in the world and there's no way he should be interested in me."

Carrielle gently pats my hand. "You underestimate your attractiveness, Jillian."

I can't help but smile. "You're very kind. But here's the big problem. I've reached the point where I cannot tell dreams from reality."

He nods. "Yes, I know. Fortunately, that's one thing I *can* fix." He touches my hand and a beautiful emerald ring appears on my ring finger. The band is gold and the stone is cut in an oval. "This will always be on your hand when you are dreaming. It does not exist anywhere else."

"Well, that's no fun. Sorry, I know this is serious."

"Jillian, when you are not sure if you are awake or dreaming, simply look at your hand. If the ring is present, it is a dream. If not, you are awake."

"Wow, that's great. Thank you, Carrielle. So what's my next move?"

The Ferris wheel brings us to the bottom as the ride comes to an end. The angel opens the door and extends his hand. "Come. We have a lot to talk about."

My eyes flicker open and Roxanne is hovering over me. "Well? Did you see the angel?"

"Yeah. We spoke for hours."

"You were out five minutes." She hands me a can of soda to get my blood sugar up, as these sessions always make me a little lightheaded. "Oh, I forgot, time has no meaning there. So what's the deal?"

I sit up and take a sip of the root beer and let the cold bubbles bathe my throat. "He gave me something so that I can tell dreams from reality. So that problem is taken care of."

"Good. What about the dream weaver?"

"Same deal as my father. Can't read her through the dark forces. But it's likely she's a minion of my father. And it's a good bet she might be manipulating Trip as well."

"So what are we supposed to do?"

"Defeat her plan."

"And that plan would be?"

"We need to figure that out first."

My stunning new client studies my face as she shakes my hand. She looks familiar. "Don't I know you?" she asks. "Are you in my Modern Lit class at Concord Hall?"

"Yeah, that's where I've seen you. So, enjoying the root canal of literature known as Moby Dick?"

"Got the Cliff Notes after the first day."

"Right there with ya."

Her name is Aspen, a honey blonde with long straight hair, ice blue eyes and classic high cheekbones. Her sleeveless blouse shows off buff shoulders and cut biceps. She's nearly as tall as Roxanne, close to six feet, with killer toned legs shown off in a short black skirt. A far cry from my usual collection of frumpy desperate housewives. I'm eager to see why a girl who looks like this needs help in the area of romance, as one would think she could have her pick of the litter. I gesture toward the chair and she takes a seat as I slide my seat in toward the crystal ball.

"So, wondering if you're gonna meet a whaler anytime soon?" I ask.

She laughs. "Yeah, I'm looking for a guy named Ishmael but there aren't a lot of those on campus. By the way, I love your hair color. Such a vivid red."

"Thank you."

"Real or bottle?"

"I come from a long line of spunky redheads."

"Well, it's gorgeous."

"Your hair is beautiful too. So, Aspen, tell me why you're here."

"Well, I went through a lot of bad relationships in high school and now that I'm around men instead of boys, I'm hoping you might point me in the right direction. Or at least keep me from moving in the wrong one, as I often go for guys who are totally bad for me. I'd like to limit the number of frogs I have to kiss before I find my prince."

"Sure, I hear ya."

"And you've gotta admit there are a lot of hot guys on campus. You hooked up with anyone yet?"

The image of Trip flashes through my mind and I quickly shove it aside. "I'm in love with my high school sweetheart, so I'm off the market."

"Hey, lucky you."

"But I do agree there's a serious amount of eye candy wandering around that campus."

I tell her to ask a specific question, then concentrate on it. I take a mental picture of Aspen, then close my eyes and focus on her. When I open my eyes the crystal ball is fogged but quickly clearing.

"You see something already?" she asks.

"Not yet, give it a minute."

The fog clears, replaced by an image which tells me it's probably December as I see snow on the windows that are bordered with holiday lights. It looks like an expensive restaurant, decorated with a Christmas tree and colorful red and green garland. Aspen is smiling as she eats her dinner. A small rectangular gold package with a red bow is pushed across the table by a man's hand and her eyes light up.

"Ah, you're out to dinner in a very nice place with a man who's giving you a Christmas present."

"Can you see who it is?"

I shake my head. "Not yet. All I saw was a man's hand and a gift box. Give me a minute."

"Geez, I hope it's a cute guy and not my dad."

I see her unwrap the gift, revealing a long jewelry box. She opens it and her jaw drops. She pulls out a gorgeous ruby necklace.

"Well, he has expensive taste. You want me to tell you what the present is?"

"No way, I like surprises. So who's my sugar daddy?"

"Don't know yet. Patience, grasshopper."

I see her hand the necklace across the table as she sits up straight and pulls her hair out of the way. She obviously wants her date to put the necklace on for her. A body in a dark gray suit moves behind her, but I cannot see the man's face. His hands move around her head, then clasp the necklace. She drops her hair as she admires it.

And then Trip Logan leans down and kisses her on the cheek.

I asked Ryan to come over and watch TV with me. At least I know the thing about not being able to tell dreams from reality is over. The Cruise Missile won't be able to mess with my head so much. I still have to get rid of that virus she planted in my subconscious, but at least I'm leveling the playing field a bit.

Ryan is on the couch, back against the armrest and legs stretched out. His mood is a little better, but he's not back to normal. I know the wheels of jealousy are still turning in his head. I come back from the kitchen with sodas and snacks, place them on the coffee table, then sit on the couch between his legs and lean back. I take his arms and wrap them around my waist. "Just hold me, okay?"

"Sounds good to me." He tightens his hug and kisses my neck.

"I have two pieces of good news, Ryan. I talked to the angel today."

"Oh?"

"Long story short, I'll now be able to tell when I'm dreaming and when I'm not."

"Well, that's a relief. So he got Cruise out of your head?"

"Not that simple, but at least I'll know when she's screwing with me. He gave me a dream sign to look for when I'm not sure. If I see a huge emerald ring on my left hand, I know I'm dreaming."

"Aw, dammit, now I'll have to return your Christmas present."

"Hey, give me all the emeralds you want. I do have another hand and several free fingers, you know."

"What's the other piece of good news?"

"A certain guy you've been worried about will shortly have a girlfriend. I saw it in a reading I did for this gal who's in my class."

His grip tightens slightly. "I... I wasn't worried about him."

I turn around, grab his face and kiss him. "Good, because you never had anything to worry about. I couldn't ask for a better man than you."

He gives a sheepish grin. "Thanks, Sparks."

"I know this has been hard on you, Ryan. But please know I love you."

"I know. I just couldn't bear to lose you."

"You're in no danger of that. And I couldn't lose you either." I lie on my side, head on his chest and get comfortable as he wraps his arms around me. I close my eyes as I slide one arm under him and hug him, wanting to savor the feeling.

But all my mind's eye can see is a bare-chested Trip Logan with Aspen the gorgeous blonde. She's taken my place, in his arms, legs wrapped around his waist, kissing him.

And the feeling I have isn't one of warmth from being in Ryan's arms.

It's one of jealousy. Trip is with another woman.

I must be dreaming.

I open my eyes and look at my hand.

The ring isn't there.

Chapter 6

So I've made a new friend. Aspen, my client from the other night who is going to take Trip Logan out of the picture with her supermodel looks, sits next to me in the back row of Modern Literature class. Everyone hates this professor, as he's nasty and constantly makes cutting remarks to any student who doesn't "get" the deep hidden meaning of a guy who wants to harpoon and kill a beautiful creature. Aspen's been cracking me up with her little notes and facial expressions as the ancient professor (who may have actually served under Captain Ahab) drones on endlessly about the great white whale. Reminds me of the first time I saw *Titanic* at home and yelled, "Just sink the damn boat!" after three hours of Leo and Kate making eyes at each other. I really wanted to interrupt the class and yell, "Just harpoon the damn whale!" but, ya know, I've read the Cliff Notes and need a decent grade.

The bell thankfully ends the monotone monologue and the class flies out of the room like the people escaping from the theater in *The Blob*.

"That class makes me want to slit my wrists," says Aspen, as we head into the hallway.

"I was thinking for my term paper I might re-write the ending, and have the whale swallow Ahab, kinda like the great white shark got Quint in Jaws. Then have a policeman blow the thing up with a rifle."

"I like it."

"How do teachers like that keep their jobs?"

She shakes her head as she pops a bubble with her gum. "Maybe he slept with someone in power. You know, back in 1930."

I like her immensely. She's incredibly smart and witty, not what you'd expect from such a serious babe. An airhead former prom queen or head cheerleader, she's not. A guy would refer to her as a total package. I'm counting on that. I mean, if Trip found *me* attractive he should go crazy when he sees Aspen.

We turn a corner and I see Trip Logan heading in our direction at the far end of the hall. Think fast. Time for a preemptive strike. "Hey, Aspen, you know the guy I saw you with in the reading?"

"Yeah?"

"You wanna meet him?"

"Of course. I thought that was a given."

"I meant, right now." I cock my head in his direction. "He's headed this way."

Her eyes widen as she looks down the hall and checks out the prospects. "Really? Which one?"

"Passing the water fountain. The huge guy in the red shirt who is off the charts hot."

Her jaw drops slightly as she spots Trip. "You gotta be kidding. *That's* the guy I'm ending up with?"

"Yep. Not exactly chopped liver, huh?"

"Wow. Damn, he is *smoking* hot. And I like 'em tall."

"C'mon, I'll introduce you."

She stops and grabs my forearm. "Wait... you know him?"

"Yeah. Met him a couple of weeks ago. He's a really nice guy."

"But... are you supposed to do this?"

"Hey, I read the future. Who's to say I'm not supposed to be the one to hook you guys up? C'mon, let's get the ball rolling."

She looks down at her outfit: skinny jeans that show off her mile long legs, boots and a tight red sweater. "But I'm not even dressed. Maybe we can set something up when I'm in a skirt."

"Trust me, girl, you'd stop traffic in a burlap sack." I take her arm and lead her down the hall. "Let's go. He'll love you. Then you can really knock his socks off when you go out."

"Okay, but you know what they say. You only get one chance to make a first impression."

Trip spots me when we're a few feet away. He nods, doesn't say anything, then looks away. He's keeping his word to avoid me.

"Hey, Trip," I say, as he's about to pass.

He stops, gives me a puzzled look. "Hello, Jillian." He quickly looks around, probably wanting to make sure Ryan isn't nearby. "I thought—"

I grab Aspen's arm and pull her toward him. "Listen, I wanted you to meet my friend Aspen. She's a nice girl, you're a nice guy... I thought you two might hit it off."

He extends his hand, shoots that incredible shy smile and her face flushes. "Pleasure, Aspen."

"Yeah, uh-huh," she says, going into a trance, the gum nearly falling out of her mouth.

"Maybe you two would like to go for coffee," I say. "Or lunch."

His eyes take a quick inventory of her body and I can tell he's interested. "Are you free?"

"I can be free," she says, turning to me and smiling. "What the hell, Economics class is overrated. Take notes for me?"

"You got it." I'll actually have to pay attention, but it's a small price to pay. "You two have a nice time. Gotta run."

"Thanks, Jillian," says Trip.

"Really," says Aspen, as she shoots me a wink.

I head down the hall with a big smile, knowing I've finally taken that hunky bit of temptation off the table. Take that, dream weaver.

As I reach the end of the hall I turn, just in time to see Trip take Aspen's arm and lead her out of the building.

And my heart drops as the green eyed monster rears its ugly head.

I'm surprised to see Fuzzball walking out of the amphitheater classroom. "Hey, Detective, what are you doing here?"

He puts an arm around my shoulders, pulls me off to the side and lowers his voice. "Bugging a certain classroom."

"Isn't that illegal?"

He gives me that look-the-other-way New Yorker wide-eyed face. "Seriously, Jillian?"

I playfully slap the side of my face. "Sorry. What the hell was I thinking?"

"Look, Sebastien already had a couple of mind readers in the class and got nothing from her. So I borrowed some surveillance gear from my friend at the FBI. I got a couple of video cameras in there. A United States Senator is going to be a guest speaker in the near future and the school thinks I'm just here doing a security sweep. Anyway, we want to compare what this teacher actually says to what Jake thinks he hears."

"I don't understand. If the mind readers got nothing—"

"They may have been under her influence being in the same room."

"Why, were they both male?"

"Nope, one guy, one gal. But she still could have been using the dream weaver thing on the woman. Anyway, she can't meld with technology, like your father could, so this will give us a better look at what she's doing."

I nod. It makes sense. "So what's the plan after you record her?"

"We're all meeting at your house tonight. So round up Ryan, Roxanne and Jake and I'll be by with the tape at seven."

Ryan calls and tells me his subway train is stuck and to start without him. Fuzzball has the video cued up on our television, while Mom and I stand in the back of the room sipping hot chocolate. Jake and Roxanne are holding hands on the couch. "Ryan's stuck on a train," I say, as I hang up. "He said not to wait 'cause he has no idea when he'll get here."

Fuzzball nods, sits in the recliner and points the remote at the television. "Okay, let's see what we've got." The video gives us a split screen view of the class; one camera is set up in the back of the room while the other is behind the teacher's desk. Students file in and take their seats, half engaged in loud conversation while the other half are obsessed with their cell phones. Their chatter subsides as Rebecca Cruise enters the room, shuts the door, moves to the desk and slides her briefcase onto it. All is quiet as she pulls out a laptop and connects it to the projector, humming a tune as she does this.

The men in the class all sit up straight while their eyes glaze over.

"What the hell?" says Mom. "She's hasn't even said anything yet."

And then I see it.

Fuzzball and Jake sitting up straight with the same look as the students on the tape. I take Mom's arm. "Mom, look at the guys."

"Yeah, I know. The whole class is in a trance."

"No, I mean the guys in *this room*. Look at their faces."

Mom moves around to the front and takes a closer look at Jake and Fuzzball. Both are wide-eyed and riveted to the screen as Ms. Cruise launches into her radical manifesto. Both nod slowly as she makes her point.

Roxanne waves her hand in front of Jake's face. "Earth to Jake!" No reaction. He doesn't even blink. "He's in contact with the mother ship."

"And apparently she only affects men," I say.

Mom takes the remote from Fuzzball and pauses the video, which seems to jolt the guys back to reality. Both start to blink quickly as they shake their heads.

"What's wrong, Zelda?" asks the detective.

"Something happened to you and Jake."

"What are you talking about?" asks Jake. "We were just watching the video."

"We should have had a camera on you two," says Mom. "You both became deer in the headlights once she started, same as the men in the video. Tell me, what was the teacher talking about?"

"Just some patriotic stuff," says Jake. "How she loves America, how we should do all we can for our country. And she has some assignments for us to prove our patriotism."

Fuzzball nods. "Yeah, same here."

Mom shakes her head. "Not exactly. Rox, what did you hear?"

"It was pretty radical," she says. "She wants to crash the system. She's as anti-America as you can get."

"Jillian?"

I nod. "Same deal."

Fuzzball's face tightens. "But this is *video* of her. She's not in the room. Jake has been close to her but I haven't. Why would it affect me?"

"And why does it only affect men?" asks Roxanne.

Mom stands up straight as her eyes widen. "Oh my God!"

"What, Mom?"

"She's not just a dream weaver," says my mother. "She's also a siren."

"A what?" asks Jake.

Fuzzball nods. "Zelda, that makes perfect sense."

"So what's a siren?" I ask.

Mom heads for the kitchen to get her encyclopedia of paranormal powers, talking as she goes. "It's from Greek mythology, but in this case it's not a myth. There have been a few documented cases." She returns with the book, flipping through the pages. "A siren is a woman who can hypnotize men with her song. And make them do whatever she wants."

"And this is bad...why?" I ask.

"Let me download that song to my iPod," says Roxanne, smiling at Jake.

"Stop kidding around, you two. The siren is a mind controller. She can also do it with her voice," says Mom. "But the song is the most powerful. You notice she was humming when she entered the classroom and all the men went into a trance. And so did the men in this room."

"Makes sense," says Fuzzball. "So she has two powers, like Jillian and her father."

"Obviously," says Mom. "Two incredibly strong powers. If she doesn't get you with one she can nail you with the other."

"Or, in some cases, both," says Fuzzball.

"So what's the legend say?" I ask.

Mom reads from the book. "Sirens could basically hypnotize sailors, make them believe things that weren't real and send them off a cliff. They're also known as the muses of the underworld."

Roxanne sits bolt upright. "Whoa, wait a minute. They're *muses*?"

"Not exactly, as their definition of inspiration isn't exactly in Webster's, since they can only inspire people to kill themselves. However, according to legend, the sirens had a war with the muses, and were defeated."

Roxanne cracks her knuckles. "So I'll just kick her ass and we'll be done with the bitch. I'm a muse. I rule."

"Probably easier said than done," says Mom. "She could still get to your dreams."

"So, she can't affect women?" I ask.

"Not as a siren. But she's still a dream weaver, so none of us is immune. However, it does give the women a little advantage in that she can only use one of her powers against us."

"Well, she can't use either against me, thanks to Carrielle," I say. I look at Roxanne and her face tells me the Sicilian revenge wheels are turning in her mind. "Now don't go all Michael Corleone on us. We need to work out a plan."

She gives me her wide-eyed innocent girl look and points at herself. "*Moi*? Would I fly off the handle and exact revenge on someone who is screwing with my boyfriend's head without thinking it through?"

"Yes," we all say in stereo.

Jake pats her on the knee. "Gotta love her attitude, though.

Ready, fire, aim. That's my girl."

An hour later after we've all had a crash course in Sirens 101, Ryan arrives. "Sorry I'm so late, guys."

I walk over to him and give him a big hug as he kisses me. "It's okay, we figured it out. And we need you to test something."

I explain the whole thing about sirens and how Jake and Fuzzball went into a trance once Cruise started humming.

"So," says Ryan, "if you guys already figured it out, what do you need me to do?"

"Have a seat," says Mom. "We're gonna try a little experiment."

"Sure."

Roxanne and Jake scoot over as Ryan and I sit on the couch. I take his hand. "Okay, watch the TV."

Mom fires the remote. The video is cued up to where we left off, and the teacher continues her radical spiel.

Ryan doesn't react. "Okay, she's a left wing whack job. We already knew that."

"She didn't seem patriotic to you?" asks Jake.

He furrows his brow. "You kidding? You thought *that* was patriotic? She sounds like she wants to blow up the White House. I'm amazed they let her teach at the college."

"Hang on a minute," says Mom. "We're not done. I think I've figured this out." She points the remote at the television, backing the video up to the beginning, then hits the play button.

The moment Ms. Cruise starts humming, Ryan sits up straight and develops the same hypnotic look we saw on Jake and Fuzzball. Mom lets the video roll for a couple of minutes, then stops it.

"I guess I misjudged her," says Ryan, still in some sort of trance. "She's quite the patriot."

"What did she say specifically that makes you say that?" asks Mom

Ryan shrugs. "I don't know. I just know I like her and she loves this country. And wants me to show my patriotism in specific ways."

"That's it," says Mom, tossing the remote on the coffee table.

"What?" I ask.

“It’s her song, not her voice. She needs music to put men in a trance.”

Chapter 7

I take a sip of the richest chocolate malt in New York City. "This is nice of you. But you didn't have to buy me lunch."

"Hey, if it weren't for you I wouldn't be dating a terrific guy," says Aspen, picking daintily at her grilled chicken salad.

I point at her lunch, which seems an odd choice for a throwback fifties diner. The deep-fried air of the place almost commands you to order something unhealthy, like my bacon cheeseburger. "That all you gonna eat?"

"I look at a French fry and gain five pounds. That's why I do weight training. I have a really slow metabolism."

"Bummer," I say, as I grab my burger and take a huge bite. "So, I take it you and Trip are hitting it off."

She flashes a naughty smile and both eyebrows go up. "You might say that."

"I *might*?"

"No, you can. We have a lot in common and a great time when we're together. He is *such* a gentleman. So old fashioned. Holds doors open for me, walks on the outside of the sidewalk. Chivalrous, you know?"

The memory of being carried to the infirmary flashes through my mind. "Actually, I do. So, things getting serious?"

She shrugs. "Jillian, he's one of those guys who moves slowly.

And I sure don't want to chase him away so I'm playing along. I mean, damn, what a catch."

"Yeah, he does seem like the total package."

She looks around to make sure no one's listening, then leans forward. "I have a confession to make. I did something a little naughty the other night."

"Really? Do tell."

"Well, my parents have an apartment in Manhattan and they were out of town, so I brought him back there after we had dinner and went to a movie. Then I used one of the oldest tricks in the book."

"And that would be?"

"I spilled a drink on his shirt."

I suck down the remainder of the malt, which is so damn good I make that supposedly embarrassing sucking sound with the straw. "Not sure I've heard of that one."

"Well, I was dying to see him with his shirt off and so I made sure he needed to change."

"Hmmm. Very clever."

"Anyway, I apologize profusely and offer to wash his shirt. He doesn't want to sit there soaking wet so he takes it off and I throw it in the washer on the slowest cycle. Oh. My. God. Jillian, you have never seen a body like the one on Trip Logan. It's like some artist drew him."

"Yeah, I kinda figured with those arms the rest of him would be pretty good."

"The boy is ripped. Two hundred and forty pounds of solid muscle."

I furrow my brow. "What'd you do, weigh him?"

She shakes her head. "Nah, he told me he's captain of the college wrestling and weight lifting teams so I looked him up on the Internet after he left. And some of his wrestling matches are on YouTube. He absolutely destroyed his opponents and he's undefeated. And he holds all the school weight lifting records."

"Well, he is a big boy."

"But I tell ya, it broke my heart when the buzzer on the dryer went off. That was ninety minutes of pure eye candy. And I love the fact he's six-five... I can wear heels around him. Had to wear flats with my last boyfriend."

"Well, I'm happy for you. And I know he's got to be attracted to you just as much."

She shrugs again. "I sure hope so."

"What, really? Aspen, you're gorgeous. Women would kill to look like you."

"Oh, there's definitely a physical attraction between us. But I can't help but get the feeling he's still hung up on someone else."

I catch up with Roxanne in the coffee bar. She's riveted to a book as I slide my drink onto the table and crane my neck to look at the cover.

"History of Greek Mythology, huh?"

"Well, *Kicking the Ass of a Siren for Dummies* was out of stock."

"So, what's it say?"

"Some of the things your mom talked about. A bunch of legends. Useful things I need to know. And there's a lot of stuff about the war between the muses and the sirens."

"The muses won, right?"

"Yeah, they kicked butt."

"How did they do it?"

"Apparently it was the equivalent of a sing-off. *American Idol* smackdown for mythological creatures. Anyway, the sirens and muses held a singing contest and the muses won." She looks at the book. "Then, and I love this part, the muses plucked the feathers from the sirens and wore them as a trophy."

"Sounds like something you'd do. Can I see that book a minute?"

She sends it across the table. "Knock yourself out. It's a helluva lot more interesting than the so-called classics we're reading in Modern Literature class."

"Speak for yourself. I'm *almost* reading. You can borrow the Cliff Notes."

I turn the book around and start to read.

Sirens are often portrayed as a combination of women and birds and are known for their beautiful but hypnotic voices. Their song can be enchanting to men, as they are said to have lured sailors to steer their ships into rocky coasts, where they would shipwreck. However, Odysseus managed to sail past he sirens by having his crew fill their ears with wax. A siren's song has no effect on females.

They are sometimes known as muses of the underworld since their motives are anything but benevolent. But they are not as powerful as the traditional muses. Legend has it that Hera conducted a singing contest between the sirens and the muses. The muses defeated the sirens so soundly that they plucked the feathers from the sirens and fashioned them into crowns, which they wore in triumph.

"Okay, so a muse can defeat a siren with song. Can you sing?"

She shakes her head. "I'm really awful. The first time I sang in church the priest came up to me after Mass and told me that God gives everyone gifts, but a good singing voice was not one I'd received."

"That bad?"

"I think he was worried I'd shatter the stained glass. Seriously, you wanna hear *Ave Maria* with my accent?"

"Not particularly."

"Then there was the time in Florida when I was outside by myself and started to sing. All the mockingbirds flew away. That's why I only sing when I'm alone in my car."

"Well, I don't think quality matters in this case. All Ms. Cruise did was hum and it sent the guys into a trance."

"True. But even though a muse trumps a siren, I can't hypnotize a man by singing."

"How do you know?"

"Tried it with Jake and it didn't work. He just begged me to stop. Said he loved me but that I made fingernails on the blackboard sound like Pavarotti by comparison."

I bookmark the page and slide the book back to her. "You do know what this means, don't you?"

She nods, suddenly turning serious. "Yeah. If we're gonna defeat the bitch, I'm the one who's ultimately going to do it. Do-re-mi."

I'm not at all wild about what's about to happen as I materialize next to Ryan outside the amphitheater. The halls are empty since class is in the middle of the period.

"Are you okay?" I ask.

"Yes, Miss Spectre," he says in a robotic voice. "Do with me what you wish. I am at your service."

I gently slap him on the arm. "Stop it, this is serious."

"Just trying to lighten the mood, Sparks. Don't worry, I got here after she was done with her singing, so she hasn't turned me into a pod person. But I wasn't kidding about letting you do whatever you want to me."

I lean up and give him a kiss. "I'll take you up on that later, Mister."

It's good to see Ryan getting back to his normal relaxed self despite the seriousness of the task at hand. I think my playing Jewish mother for Trip and Aspen has put him at ease. While Ryan's a confident guy, I can see how any man would see Trip Logan as a threat, especially after seeing me wrapped around him like a party bimbo at the dance. (Hey, if I saw him making out with a babe like Aspen, I'd probably react the same way.)

But right now I'm the worried one, as he's about to read the mind of Ms. Cruise, since his powers have been "altered" according to Sebastien. The Council is hoping Ryan might have better luck than the female mind readers they sent. And even though they had no ill effects from visiting the class, I'm playing it safe by being here just in case he needs to be healed.

I peek through the window and see the teacher holding court, men in a trance as she paces back and forth. She stops walking, hops up on the desk right in front of Jake and crosses her legs. Her skirt rides high on her thigh as the men begin to drool. Jake's eyes bug out and I can tell he's under her spell.

"Let's do this before she goes all full metal cougar on Jake."

He nods and peeks through the window. "No kidding."

"Before we start, let me ask you a question. Do you find her attractive?"

He shrugs. "She's okay. I mean, she looks damn good for her age but I've never been into older women. Though I can see how she could turn into a praying mantis if she were a shape shifter."

"Interesting way to put it."

"She mates, she kills. If we're done discussing my lack of attraction to age-inappropriate women, I'm ready."

"Okay, but the minute you feel anything out of the ordinary, stop."

"Don't worry, I will."

"Yeah, right. You always think you're bulletproof."

"I take after a certain redhead."

"Funny. C'mon, let's get it over with."

He moves closer to the door so the teacher will be in his range, peeks through the window, and I take his hand. He turns to me with a reassuring look. "Sparks, I'll be okay."

"Just in case you need a dose of life force, I wanna be in place."

"Sure. Okay, let me concentrate."

He closes his eyes and I squeeze his hand tight while watching his face. If I see any reaction, I'm pulling the plug on this operation. But his expression doesn't change. He nods slightly, keeping his eyes closed. I can tell he's getting something. I begin to relax my grip. He squeezes my hand and smiles. After a few minutes he furrows his brow and starts to grow pale.

"You okay, Ryan?"

"Shhhh. Fine. Let me concentrate."

I shut up, but keep a close eye on him. A minute later he opens his eyes.

"Okay, done. See, no side effects."

I give him a strong hug. "Thank God." I pull back, look up at him and see the worry in his eyes. "I can tell you got something bad."

"Yeah. Sebastien's right, my abilities must have slightly changed. That was a really clear reading. She's different than anyone I've ever read."

"How so?"

"It's almost like part of her mind has a wall up that I can't get through. Still, I made some progress."

"Well, don't keep me in suspense."

"It'll take me quite a while to tell you everything, but I got two big things. It turns out that your mother was right. She's a siren."

"Makes sense. But that's not what upset you. What's the other biggie?"

The color drains from his face.

"What? Ryan, what did you see?"

"It's really hard for me to tell you this, considering Rox is your best friend." He takes my shoulders and looks into my eyes. "She once killed a muse."

It's the biggest collection of people I've ever seen in one room at The Summit. Sebastien is here with the entire council, as are Roxanne, Jake, my mother, Fuzzball, and me. Ryan is in the hot seat, that throne-like chair I was in when they first questioned me. The serious looks on the faces of the powers that be tell me we're facing the same kind of trouble we had with my father. I guess I was naive to think we were over and done with the forces of evil once we committed him to the coma, but when you step back and look at the empire he built, it's only natural that he'd have his followers.

Followers who apparently want to continue his work.

And while we know his original plan was to destroy faith, we don't know what he planned to do afterward.

As for Ms. Cruise and her history with muses, we haven't told Roxanne yet. Sebastien wants to deal with that later without the rest of The Council present. She knows something's up since I've apparently been evasive. But when you're worried your best friend might have to go up against someone so powerful, it's only natural that you'd seem different. To say I've lost sleep over this is putting it mildly. Sebastien assures me he'd never put her in danger, but by now you know Roxanne.

"Let's begin," says Sebastien, who gets up from the long table filled by seven other council members. "Ryan, let's go through what you gathered from Ms. Cruise, and don't leave out even the smallest detail."

"Sure," says Ryan. "Right away I could tell she was different than anyone I'd ever read. I could only access part of her mind. Part of her subconscious seemed to be locked away."

"Very well," says Sebastien. "Continue."

"She definitely has the powers of a siren. She starts each class and any conversation she wants to control by humming, and the legend is true that she can only control men."

"What is her objective?"

"That part I couldn't get, but I did discover that she was working closely with Jillian's father and admired him a great deal. She wants to continue his work and is part of a group committed to doing that. Unfortunately I couldn't get any names, so I have no idea who she is working with. She knows who took down J.T. Decker, and she is determined to drive a wedge between us. But I don't think she knows Jillian is in contact with an angel, or that she can now tell the difference between dreams and reality. They still think they can manipulate her that way."

"What about her abilities as a dream weaver?"

Ryan shakes his head. "I got nothing, except the group feels that confusing dreams and reality is a good way to drive us apart. And Ms. Cruise is definitely going to try to seduce Jake."

Roxanne cracks her knuckles, the sound echoing through the room. "Bring it, Mrs. Robinson."

"Do you think she's the one who contacted Jillian's father?"

"I didn't pick up anything specific. But she does know he's been contacted."

"Any idea why?"

Ryan shakes his head. "No. But they plan to do it again. And soon."

Every member of The Council reacts, eyebrows going up, eyes growing wide.

"What about the ultimate plan?" asks Sebastien.

"This was the part that scared me, Sebastien. They feel confident they can finish what Decker started, using mind control. But the thing with the cell phone was only the first part of his master plan."

"And the second part would be?"

Ryan's face suddenly goes pale. "I don't know. But the phrase I picked up was, 'This will only be the beginning. And then we can fulfill Decker's dream.'"

Fuzzball is next, and he pulls a bunch of manila envelopes from his briefcase. "As you know, Ms. Cruise is well connected in the area of politics, having served a couple of terms in Congress. She serves as an adjunct professor at the college and only teaches two classes. Which leaves her plenty of time for other activities." He moves to The Council's table, then hands each member a manila envelope. "This is her dossier from Homeland Security. Most of it contains things that are well known. She's still a close adviser to the governor and one of our United States Senators. What is most interesting are her activities that are off the grid." He smiles and winks at me. "Well, make that activities she *thinks* are off the grid."

He moves to our table and hands out the envelopes. "A lot of this is political, her voting record, activities before and after she served in Congress. She participated in a lot of radical protests when she was in college. And she was involved with a lot of men when she was in Congress." I get the last envelope and pull out the folder. Fuzzball locks eyes with me and I know something bad is inside. "But if you'll turn to the back page, I think the photo will explain a lot."

I flip to the back and the eight-by-ten black-and-white photo makes my jaw drop.

A very young Rebecca Cruise, probably in her early twenties.

Holding hands with my father.

Mom is quiet as we sit in a conference room waiting for Sebastien. She hasn't said a word since Fuzzball passed out the folders. Obviously the photo of my father with another woman is bothering her, and I know the question that is going through her mind. Because it's the same one going through mine.

Was the photo taken before he moved out?

And if so, what was his relationship with the woman? I mean, it could have been anything, as the photo shows them sitting on a park bench. Not terribly close, not looking like they were in love or even *friends with benefits*, but holding hands nonetheless. Could be one person comforting another. Or something much more.

Mom told me he wasn't the kind of guy to have an affair, that they were madly in love, but then again she never would've guessed the guy she married would turn out to be a deadbeat dad and disciple of hell.

It only makes me hate the guy even more.

He's close to someone who killed a muse. Of all the people with paranormal powers, muses are by far the most gentle, benevolent creatures in how they use their gifts to create such great beauty. If you're into fantasy, it's almost like taking the life of a unicorn.

Meanwhile, Roxanne is about to be told the whole story about the siren from hell and that her life is most likely in danger. I'm sitting next to her, knowing she'll get emotional when she gets the news. Emotional good or emotional bad, we'll soon find out.

Sebastien enters the room, looking upset, then sits down

opposite Roxanne.

She looks at his long face and knows immediately something is wrong. "What?"

Sebastien folds his hands and rests them on the table. "Roxanne, legend has it that a siren can be defeated by a muse."

"Right."

"You must remember that some legends are merely that. Greek mythology is often what it claims to be."

"Well, a muse is supposed to be a mythological creature and I'm not a myth. So it has some basis in fact."

"Yes, very true. The same holds true for a siren. And now a dream weaver. But while the mere existence of those with such powers would seem to confirm legend, we do not know for certain if the stories concerning those are completely accurate. We do not know which are true and which are simply ancient lore. So we must be objective."

"I'm not sure what you're getting at."

Sebastien turns to Ryan. "Tell her, Ryan."

Ryan bites his lower lip, looks at the table, then up at Roxanne. "Rox, there was one thing I left out when I told The Council about what I'd picked up when I read Cruise's mind. It's about you."

"Yeah, you told us that she knew we were the ones who took down Jillian's father."

"It's more than that, Rox," I say, taking her hand.

"What?" she asks.

Ryan exhales deeply. "It's not about you specifically, but about muses. The legend about the muses defeating the sirens... it's not necessarily true in real life. Cruise went up against a muse once before, many years ago."

"And...?"

Ryan looks at me, eyes filled with anguish, then back at her. "The muse didn't come out of it alive."

I expect Roxanne's jaw to drop, for the color to drain from her face, but this doesn't happen. She says nothing and nods for a moment, processing what she just heard. Then she turns to Sebastien. "Well, then, I guess we need to find out who she killed and why the muse couldn't defeat her. Get all the specifics. Then figure out what we can do so it doesn't happen again."

"You're kidding me," I say.

"What?"

"Did what Ryan told you even remotely register in that stubborn head of yours?"

Roxanne nods. "Yeah. I get it. The woman is dangerous and has no qualms about killing people. I would expect that since she was in cahoots with your father, and he had no problem trying to kill us either. So I realize we need to be careful. What the hell do you expect me to say? That I'm afraid to take her on? Because I'm not. You're not the only girl in the neighborhood who can save the planet, you know."

Finally Jake chimes in as he takes her hand. "Rox, I'm not prepared to lose you. We'll find another way."

She shakes her head. "No. Suppose the only person who can defeat this particular siren is a muse? And suppose, since my talents have been slightly altered, that I'm the only muse with the power to do it? What then? We just let her continue what Jillian's father started? Sorry, ain't gonna happen."

No one says anything for a minute. Sebastien leans back in his chair and rests his hands in his lap. "I know this is going to be an unpopular statement with this group, but I am inclined to agree with Roxanne."

Chapter 8

Ryan and I are headed to the coffee bar when we see them.

Ms. Cruise (now referred to as Mrs. Robinson) and Jake.

She has her hand lightly on his shoulder. Dressed in her usual age inappropriate short skirt and sky-high heels, it's clear what she has in mind as she licks her lips.

He's wearing the deer-in-the-headlights look, in contact with the mother ship.

They're heading in our direction, which is also the direction of her office. And, quite possibly, what I saw in my reading.

I grab Ryan's forearm. "Ryan, we gotta stop this. Jake's not even in his body. If she gets him to her office—"

"I know, I can see it too. I'm on it."

Ryan picks up his pace as they grow closer. I continue slowly walking toward them, but try to blend in with the crowd and move close to the wall.

"Hey, Jake!" yells Ryan as he trots toward them. "Dude, where ya been? Did you forget?"

Jake looks at Ryan as if he doesn't recognize him. "Forget what?"

"Tickets for today's Mets game." He takes Jakes arm. "C'mon, man, I paid a lot for these."

Jake studies his face. "We've got tickets to the game?"

Ryan raises his hand to his head, pretending to rub his forehead to hide the fact he's closing his eyes for a moment. It's what he does when he wants to do a quick mind read. "Yeah. What, didja get your dates mixed up?" He puts his hand down. "C'mon, let's go. Gotta catch the number seven express train." Ryan literally yanks Jake away from the teacher, who is left there dumbfounded. Then she looks pissed off.

I immediately turn away before she has the chance to see me and head quickly out of the building. My cell gives its chime that indicates a text message. I pull it out, see it's from Ryan, and am directed to a meeting place.

Jake is still shaking the cobwebs out of his head when I arrive at the entrance to the park across the street from the campus. "You okay?

"I think so. I don't even remember how I got out of the classroom."

I look at Ryan. "Did you get a read on her?

"Yeah. She was gonna do it," says Ryan. "Today was the day. And damn, is she pissed at me."

"Yeah, I'll bet. Hell hath no fury like a sex-starved siren scorned."

"Roxanne would've killed me," says Jake.

"Nah," I say, patting him on the shoulder, "she would have killed your teacher. She knows you're not in control around the siren."

"We need to call Sebastien," says Ryan as we all take seats on a large park bench under a huge maple tree. "Jake can't possibly stay in that class. I know Sebastien wanted to keep him there to let her think we weren't onto her, but that ship has sailed."

"Agreed," I say.

A woman's scream from across the street makes me whip my head around. "What the hell was that?" A crowd is gathering in front of the campus, with everyone looking up.

"What's going on?" asks Ryan.

Jake points up at the roof. "It's a jumper."

Sure enough, a guy in a business suit is on the roof of the building, right on the edge. I hear a siren in the distance (the police car kind, not the evil bitch from hell kind), growing closer. "I'm not sure I wanna watch this," I say, noting half the crowd has their cell phones pointed at the guy, hoping to capture video of the fall and the inevitable splat followed by the upload to YouTube.

Jake shades his eyes and squints at the man. "Oh, wow. I know who that is."

"Who?" asks Ryan.

"It's the guest speaker from Cruise's class today. Senator Parker."

I look again at the roof and, sure enough, it really is the United States Senator from New York, Frank Parker. The guy is walking on the edge of the roof, looking down. A few people in the crowd are actually urging him to jump, obviously not valuing the life of a politician.

The siren gets louder, and a fire department ladder truck pulls up in front of the building. "You think they got a ladder to reach the roof?" I ask.

The question becomes moot as the Senator sticks his arms straight out in front of him and casually jumps off the roof as if he were diving into a swimming pool. The crowd screams as his body falls. Ryan grabs my head and turns it around so I can't watch and holds me tight, but I can't avoid the sound of the sickening thud as his body slams into a car.

I start to turn around but Ryan takes my hand and leads me away. "You don't need to look at this, Sparks."

"I'm sorry I watched," says Jake. "Won't be able to get that image out of my head."

We start walking toward the other end of the park. "You think this has anything to do with pulling Jake out of there?" I ask.

"I do," says Ryan. "I think Cruise is showing us what she's capable of."

The headline blared from the front page:

RISING POLITICAL STAR FALLS TO DEATH

New York's junior Senator Frank Parker, one of the up and coming members of the U.S. Senate, took his own life when he jumped off a building in Lower Manhattan.

Parker, 48, had been in town as a guest speaker for a political science class taught by adjunct professor Rebecca Cruise, herself a former member of Congress and a longtime friend of the Senator. Shortly after the class he apparently made his way to the roof, walked on the edge for a few moments, then jumped off. He fell ten stories and landed on a parked car.

College student Trip Logan ran to the Senator and said he was still conscious after the fall. "He looked at me like he was really confused, took my hand and asked me 'What happened?'" said Logan. "Then he closed his eyes and stopped breathing. The paramedics got there a few seconds later but they couldn't revive him."

Curious last words for a man who seemed to be on the fast track to the White House.

Cruise said Parker seemed in good spirits during his classroom visit. "He was enjoying the give and take with the class, having fun, and the students really enjoyed meeting an active member of the U.S. Senate. I had no indication that anything was wrong, and I've known Frank a long time. We talk quite often and had planned to have dinner after the class."

Cruise and Parker had often worked together on bills in Congress during her terms there. "He was a good man and a good friend. The country lost a very bright mind today."

As for Parker's replacement, his death is too close to the end of his term and therefore filling the seat cannot be done through a special election. Governor Ted Rapter will appoint someone to fill out his term, but obviously will not do so until after Parker's funeral this weekend.

My hands are shaking as I close the newspaper and put it on the coffee table. Mom is sipping tea, staring out the front window. She's been this way lately, not talking much and looking at nothing in particular, ever since she saw that old photo of my father and Cruise. But this latest development has taken things up a notch. I get up from the couch, walk over to her and slide one arm around her waist. "Mom, I'm scared."

She nods as she puts an arm across my shoulders and pulls me close. She's still staring straight ahead. "You should be, honey."

"For God's sake, she killed one of her friends to make a point."

"She's ruthless. Obviously nothing will stand in her way."

"Except us."

"Yeah. Except us." She runs her hand across my hair. "It's a real bitch being a superhero charged with saving the world, isn't it?"

"Superheroine. A female superhero is a superheroine."

"Whatever. I prefer to think of you as my kick-ass daughter."

"I like that. Did you read the whole article? Because I noticed something."

"Yeah, I read it. Why, what did you see?"

"His last words. He asked what happened. And now that I think about it, he stuck his arms out and jumped like someone off a diving board. Like he thought he could fly. Would that explain his last words?"

"It would. If he thought he was dreaming and it was possible to fly." She takes a sip of her tea. "I noticed something too. That guy who saved you, Trip whatsisname was in the story."

"Yeah, he's apparently a Boy Scout."

"He still a distraction?"

I shake my head. "Nah. I fixed him up with a gorgeous blonde after I saw them getting along really well in her reading. Though I'm sure Ms. Cruise will send him into my dreams or try to get us together when I think I'm dreaming."

"I'm glad he's out of the picture. You've got enough to worry about right now."

I move around in front of her and see a look I've never seen. Eyes narrowed, filled with hate. "Mom, you okay?"

"No, honey. I'm pissed off."

I'm walking on a beach, its sand warm and white as sugar. Waves gently lap the shore, sending cool water onto my feet. Thankfully I'm wearing a hat since the sun is strong and redheads burn very easily. But I'm also decked out in a very skimpy black string bikini; actually a thong. And since I'm not a fan of butt floss (after the great sunburned ass incident of 2011) and don't care to wear anything this revealing, I know something's not quite right.

I look down at my hand, and Carrielle's emerald ring is there, beautifully reflecting the sunlight.

Fine, I'm dreaming. No wonder I look like a cheap slut. (Though I must say I do look good.)

Now, is this a plain old dream or one planted by the dream weaver?

I'm not sure, so I continue walking down the beach. It's not terribly crowded as I weave my way through the blankets. I hear eighties music in the distance, and the smell of grilled beef wafts by from a family cooking out.

Then I see Ryan about fifty feet away, propped up on his elbows, looking out at the ocean as he sips a soda. I pick up the pace and he turns to me as I approach, but he's not happy to see me. "Uh... you're not supposed to be here."

"Why not?"

His eyes grow wide. "I... uh..."

"Hey, Ryan!" A female voice cuts through the air. I turn in its direction and see a stunning, ridiculously stacked leggy blonde running toward us. She's spilling out of a bikini top that's about two sizes too small, and Ryan beams as he locks onto her boobs, which are bouncing so much she'd get whiplash in real life. He stands up to greet her and she wraps an arm around Ryan's waist, then glares at me. "Who the hell is this?"

I fold my arms and shoot her the death stare. "I'm his *girlfriend*. He's in love with *me*."

Her eyes narrow. "Uh, Ryan's moved on." She turns to him and starts kissing him, then turns back to me. "You can go now." She waves her hand at me like she's shooing a fly.

"You're the one who's moving on, because you're not real. Get lost." I snap my fingers and the blonde slowly disappears, head to toe, like a digital photo being deleted. "Damn, that was easy."

Then I take her place.

Ryan smiles, puts his arms around me, starts to run his hands down my back—

Then, dammit, I wake up.

I'm sitting in the back row of Modern Literature class next to Aspen, dreading the next hour of mind-numbing literary whale watching, when Jake slides into the desk on my other side. He's got that devilish gleam in his eye I haven't seen since his bad boy days of wicked practical high school jokes and I know he's going to do something devious.

I lean over to him and whisper in his ear. "You're not in this class. What are you up to?"

"Oh, just lightening the mood around here. Ryan told me you'd been depressed lately and needed cheering up."

"So why did he send you?"

"He doesn't have this particular skill set."

"And what would said skill set be?"

He flashes an ear to ear grin. "I'm sure you can figure it out."

"Will I enjoy this?"

"Oh, I guarantee it."

The bell rings as our ancient Modern Literature teacher, Professor Ball, enters the room and closes the door. (As luck would have it, I found out the guy is retiring after this semester.

So I'm stuck in his very last class.) He puts his dog-eared copy of Moby Dick on the desk and grabs a piece of chalk. Ball, who must be close to eighty, has enough wrinkles to tie up a dry cleaner for a day, a shock of white hair, and eyebrows which stick straight out about an inch from his face and remind me of a mountain range. He slides his half glasses down his nose and begins his monologue in a voice that sounds like he swallowed gravel. "Let's discuss Chapter Seven."

His words fade into the background as Jake gives me a gentle elbow and points to an empty desk on the other side of the room. I look at it, not seeing anything out of the ordinary, then shrug. He taps the underside of his own desk, and now I see it.

A small CD player taped under the desk.

My eyes grow wide as I wonder what sort of musical interlude he has planned. I sit up straight for the first time in this class as I don't want to miss this. Before Jake cleaned up his act, his torment of teachers in high school was legendary, so I'm sure he's got something special planned. And since I can't stand this instructor, I'm looking forward to it.

The teacher starts to write on the board. "Now, what is Ahab thinking at this point of the book?"

Jake raises one finger, points it at the CD player, and I see a red light turn green. A sound effect fills the room.

Ba-duh. Ba-duh.

The class snickers as the Professor turns around. "Did someone have a comment?"

No one answers. Lips are bitten around the room as students try to keep from laughing, now aware of the fact that the guy who loves the story of the great white whale is not familiar with the theme from the movie *Jaws*. In-credible.

Professor Ball turns back to the board. "Is he getting close to the whale?"

Jake points his finger.

Ba-duh. Ba-duh.

"Sounds like the whale is getting closer to *him*," says a student in the front. The class snickers.

The teacher stops for a second, shakes his head and continues. "Again, is Moby Dick on his mind?"

Bum-bum-bum-bum-bum-bum-BA-DA-DUMMMMMMM!!!!!

The class can't hold it in any longer and explodes in laughter. I'm busting a gut, Aspen is doubled over with tears in her eyes and Jake is trying his best to look innocent, hands folded on his desk, sitting up straight.

The teacher places the chalk on the blackboard ledge. "Where is that infernal noise coming from?"

BUM-BUM-BUM-BUM-BUM-BUM...BUM!!!!

The class has totally lost it and will be gone for the rest of the period. Jake quickly uses his powers to free the CD player, zip it around the back of the room and into his book bag.

The professor slowly moves toward the source of the sound, looks everywhere and can't find anything.

Everyone is howling, looking at the teacher as he tries in vain to find the source. Jake points his finger toward the front of the room. The projection screen mounted above the blackboard unfurls, rolls down. And what's on it makes my jaw drop as I cover my mouth with one hand. "Oh my God, Jake, you didn't."

"I can neither confirm nor deny anything. As you know, New York is loaded with graffiti artists."

Professor Ball throws up his hands. "Well, I give up," he says. He turns to head back to the front of the room and is stopped dead in his tracks.

A well done drawing fills the projection screen. Captain Ahab's back to the whale, which has its mouth open, ready to nail him in the ass.

The caption reads, "Bite Me."

The professor's eyes narrow. "This. Is. Sac-ril-ege!"

The class continues to howl.

He marches to the front of the room, rolls the screen back up, turns and glares at the class. "I don't have to take this after fighting in the war!"

"Which side?" asks Jake. "North or South?"

The class explodes in laughter again.

The teacher stares daggers at Jake. (Who, you'll remember, isn't even in his class.) "You children are... impossible!" He heads for the door, leaves the room and slams it.

Ten minutes later a man in a suit opens the door, asks the graduate assistant to come out in the hall. They talk briefly, then the grad assistant comes back into the room and closes the door. "I've just been told that Professor Ball has tendered his resignation and I've been asked to teach the remaining classes in this course." He moves to the desk, grabs the copy of Moby Dick and holds it up. "Anyone here wanna keep talking about this shit?"

A chorus of "no!" erupts and he tosses it in the trash.

“So, since this is Modern Literature, what’s it gonna be? Hunger Games or Harry Potter?”

Chapter 9

Mom is staring at the evening news as I walk in the door, which surprises me since she's usually tuned in to either a shopping network or watching one of those Lifetime movies in which the woman scorned gets even. (Roxanne's Sicilian mother has rubbed off on her.) "Come watch this," she says, as I close the door behind me.

"Why, what's going on?" I look at the screen, filled with the face of a New York fembot anchor-babe. (Personally I think they're all holograms, part of the Borg collective, or Cylons.) The graphic over her shoulder features a photo of the now deceased Senator Frank Parker, with the word "replacement" under the photo.

"The Governor is appointing someone to fill Parker's term."

"Already? Geez, he's not even cold."

"Did you really think politicians are human beings? Besides, I'm sure his soul is on the elevator headed down."

I've never been terribly interested in politics, and have always thought most politicians are pond scum, so I shrug. "Anyway, why do I care? They're all a bunch of crooks."

"Wait till you see who it is. Trust me, you'll care."

I take off my jacket, hang it on the coat rack near the door and slide onto the couch next to her as the video dissolves to a live shot from the State Capitol in Albany. Governor Ted Rapter, a tall, burly guy in his late fifties with salt-and-pepper hair and the requisite jowls that seem to be part of any good-ole-boy politician, steps to the podium.

And then my jaw drops as a familiar face moves into the shot and stands next to him. "You gotta be kidding me! He's appointing *her*?"

Mom slowly nods as college professor and siren from hell Rebecca Cruise flashes a megawatt smile for the cameras. "The good news is your school is losing a dream weaver and a siren as a teacher. The bad news is she's getting political power. Which may have been the plan all along."

We watch intently as the Governor first talks about the great loss the state and the country have suffered with the death of Senator Swan Dive (who got a nine-point-five from the Russian judge) but insists life goes on and it is imperative that the seat be filled as quickly as possible. Then he introduces Cruise, highlighting the fact that she has already served in Congress, knows the lay of the land in Washington and holds the same basic beliefs as the Senator she killed by convincing him he could fly and sending him head first into a Chrysler minivan.

She steps to the podium, greets the crowd, then talks about her plans for the future. Her smile morphs into a serious look. "I have to say I'm not happy about the reason I'm here today. Frank Parker was an old and dear friend and I've been devastated by his loss. But since we've always been on the same page politically, I'll do my best to continue the work he started, and always keep him in mind when introducing new legislation. Those who voted for him should know very little will change." She concludes her short remarks, takes a few questions, then turns things back over to the governor.

Mom hits the mute button when the story ends.

"Mom, do you think all this was set in motion when Ryan pulled Jake away from her? So she could make her point?"

"Could be. She may have realized she'd been outed and had done all the damage she could do. She's already done something to your head and probably knew seducing Jake was off the table. So she moved onto Plan B."

"Just like that? She decides to kill someone in a few minutes? Someone she says was a close friend?"

"These people play hardball, sweetie. That guy was just collateral damage. Your father had no respect for human life, why should any of his followers? Besides, she's killed before, so this is nothing new for her."

"So what do we do now?"

"Not sure. I think the next move is hers. It may be in our best interest to see what she's up to."

"If she can affect the public with song via the television, all she'd have to do is sing."

"She doesn't have to affect the public. If she can control the media, that may be all she needs because people are a bunch of sheep who believe whatever they see on TV. Baa, baa, baa. And it might be a stronger strategy than what your father had with that cell phone. Or..."

"Or, what?"

"This might be part of his original endgame."

The gloves are now off.

Rebecca Cruise, now United States Senator Rebecca Cruise, is in Washington today, having taken the oath of office this morning.

So it's time to get pro-active and take the initiative. Sorry, Mom, but the hell with waiting for her to make the next move. Fuzzball and I are teaming up on one of our investigations, only this isn't a paying gig.

We're going to project ourselves and find out all we can on the Cruise Missile. He's going to be the fly on the wall in her Senate office while I'm going to zap myself over to her New York townhouse and do some digging. She's out of town so I should have plenty of time to go through everything, though my main objective is her computer. Since technology was my father's thing, the thinking is that she's got plenty of digital information. Mom is keeping an eye on our actual selves while we're out of our bodies.

Fuzzball takes the reclining chair while I stretch out on the couch.

"Just stay away from the windows," he says. "She lives alone so you don't want to spook the neighbors into thinking there's a burglar in the house."

"Copy that," I say, saluting him as I get into detective mode.

"And I don't think her little boytoys will be hanging around with her out of town," he says.

"How long will you be gone?"

"Till I get what I need. Anyway, you ready?"

"Yeah, let's rock."

Mom heads to the kitchen. "Good luck, you two."

Fuzzball closes his eyes and I know he's off on the DC astral projection shuttle. Frankly, it's amazing to me that he can go such a long distance. I do the same, focusing on the photos I've seen of her home from a real estate brochure Fuzzball dug up.

I materialize in the living room. I don't turn on the lights, as I don't want to do anything that might make neighbors suspicious. But there's plenty of natural light filtering through various windows, so I can see fine. The room is professionally decorated but doesn't look lived in. A brown leather couch and matching love seat dominate the room, accented by a couple of oak end tables, a coffee table and an antique secretary. A large framed print of Monet's water lilies is the only thing on the wall. It's one of those living rooms "for show" that never gets used. I flip open the secretary's top and look in the drawers but it's empty, obviously a decorative piece.

With absolutely nothing of use here, I leave the room and move down a long hallway and find what is obviously her bedroom. A king-sized four poster bed, matching nightstand, and a beige wing-backed chair fill this room. I can't resist, so I open the door to her walk-in closet and rummage through the racks. One side is filled with professional clothes, which is probably the stuff she'll wear now that she's back in the public eye. The other side features her cougar seduction fall collection: an age-inappropriate wardrobe comprised of ridiculously short skirts, revealing dresses, various spandex items and a bunch of stiletto heels. But no computer, no papers, no books of any kind other than a legal thriller on the nightstand.

The kitchen offers nothing of interest, and considering the oven looks as though it's never been used I'm going to assume she doesn't cook. Big shocker there. The fridge is bare, without the usual children's crayon drawings or photos.

The guest room offers nothing of use either. The tour of the first floor complete, I head up the very creaky hardwood stairs and find what I've been looking for.

Her office.

The strong smell of cigarette smoke hits me as I enter.

A large oak desk sits in the center of the room, illuminated by a large circular window in the center of an exposed brick wall.

And there's a laptop computer on the desk.

I slide into the leather swivel rocker behind the desk. I flip open the laptop and hit the power button.

The stale tobacco smell is awful so I shove the marble ashtray filled with butts to the far end of the desk next to a copper lighter in the shape of the State of Liberty.

I drum my fingers on the desk as the laptop hums to life, hoping the thing isn't password protected.

The screen on the laptop clears, and thankfully it isn't.

Since I'm not sure what I'm looking for and could be here all day, Fuzzball has taught me a technique by which the whole contents can be copied and emailed without any record showing up on her computer. (The stuff our government can do is scary, though, in this case, very useful.) I go through the steps and send countless gigabytes to the secure address at The Summit. Take that, bitch.

I can't help but smile, knowing my main objective has been

completed. But there could still be more, so I decide to continue searching the rest of the house. When I get up from the chair, what I see stops me dead in my tracks.

A framed photo sitting on the credenza near the window.

Rebecca Cruise is much younger, in her early twenties, laying in a bed, hair matted, no makeup, looking exhausted but smiling, as she holds a baby.

It's obvious she's just given birth.

And standing behind her, wearing a huge smile, is a man.

My father.

My jaw clenches as I grab the photo. I study it, the looks on their faces much different than the other photo I was shown at The Summit. Where the other picture showed people who might have been friends, this shows something much more. I turn the frame over, and start removing the photo.

Not because I can take it with me, because I can't. I want to see if there's a date on the back.

The loud distinctive metal click of a deadbolt turning makes me stop. I hear voices from the first floor, a door close, then two sets of footsteps heading up the creaky stairs.

My hair stands on end as I quickly put the photo back in its frame and on the credenza.

A light in the hallway turns on.

My last thought before I disappear isn't one of hate for my father.

It's that I might have a half-sibling.

I'm pacing in the living room like a caged animal, waiting for Fuzzball while trying not to explode with the information I've stumbled upon. But I need to unload this on someone, and soon.

Ninety long minutes later Fuzzball finally opens his eyes. I haven't told Mom about what I've learned, nor am I sure if I should. I know the revelation would hurt her. Especially if my father was having an affair before he left us.

As for the possible half-sibling, I'm not even sure how I feel.

It's too much, too soon. But, as you've come to learn, that's pretty much the norm when it comes to me.

Fuzzball rubs his eyes as he flips the lever on the recliner and returns to a sitting position. He turns to me, "Oh, you're back already."

"Been back for an hour and a half."

"How'd you make out?"

"We lucked out. Her computer wasn't password protected, and I copied everything like you told me, but I couldn't stay long."

"Why not? She's in D.C."

"She is, but someone with access to her house isn't. A few minutes after I got there I heard two people enter the place."

"Do you know who it was?"

I shake my head. "Nope. I was upstairs in her office. I heard people coming up the stairs and I needed to get out of there before they saw me."

"Well, at least you got the computer, that's huge. You're an honorary member of the CIA. You're a girl in black."

"Thanks, but I'll pass on that title. What'd you get?"

"A few things, but not much. She was basically getting introduced to Frank Parker's staff, so she wasn't alone for long. But when she was, she made a phone call that was interesting. She told the person on the other line to make contact with your father Saturday night."

"Do you know who it was?"

He shakes his head. "No. She covers her tracks well. The number didn't show up on her cell and I couldn't hear the voice on the other end, not that it would have told us much. Besides, it was a ten second phone call, and it was obvious she was giving the order. But what we can take from this is that she's not the person who has been contacting him."

"But if she's a dream weaver, doesn't it make sense it would be her?"

"You might think that, but it could simply be a very powerful mind reader. Remember, your father isn't necessarily dreaming, he's in a coma. Anyway, Jillian, we'll figure it out. At least we know exactly when your father will be contacted."

"Detective, there's something else—"

Mom walks into the room carrying a pitcher of lemonade, so I clam up. "I heard you guys talking. Good trip, detective?"

"I got some very useful stuff. Cruise is not the one contacting Jillian's father."

"Hmmm. Interesting." She puts the pitcher on the coffee table and begins pouring glasses. "Well, we knew she wasn't working alone."

Fuzzball nods as she hands him a glass and he takes a sip. "Yeah, but we still don't know who she's working with."

I walk Fuzzball out to his car as I need to get away from my mother. "Detective, I found something else. Something I didn't want to tell you in front of my mom." I tell him about the photo, and the implications. I'm concerned he held something back on the photo he brought to The Summit. "I was wondering if that photo you got from the feds had a date on it."

He looks me right in the eye and I know he's not trying to hide anything. "Sorry, Jillian, it was something taken from his home after you guys fried him. I take it there was no date on the photo you saw tonight."

"I was about to take it out of the frame to check when I was interrupted."

"Well, it could be something as innocent as him visiting a friend in the hospital."

"Nice try, Fuzzball. I know two people in love when I see it. He looked like a very proud father. Same as he did in the photo holding me."

"Look, kid, don't take it so hard. Your father was not a nice person. But you have a great mom and a lot of people who love you."

"Yeah, I know. Deep down I guess I'd still like to meet the guy mom fell in love with."

"That's understandable, but he no longer exists. Anyway, I guess we'll have to do some more investigating on their relationship if you're going to be able to sleep nights. I'll put one of my guys on it. If the child was born in this country there will be a record of it. But with your father's assets, they could have easily gone abroad and kept it quiet. Or the records could have been deleted. She was in politics before, so the last thing she'd need would be a record of a love child. But if your father does have a kid out there, we need to find that person. It might be a big part of the equation, it might not. And there's something else we need to consider."

"What's that?"

"Your father has two powers and so does Cruise. If they actually did have a child together, can you imagine what their offspring would possess?"

To say I'm in shock is putting it mildly as Roxanne and I breathe in the sugary air of her family's pastry shop. I've already wolfed down one cannoli and am considering another. Check that, I'm considering a third. I've already decided on a second.

"You tryin' to make the weight?" asks Roxanne.

"I'm stressed. Leave me alone and get me more pastry." I clap my hands. "Chop chop."

"Demanding little redhead, aren't you? Though you won't be little for long if you keep this up." She shakes her head, gets up, walks behind the counter, and returns with a second cannoli. This one is dipped in chocolate. "Knock yourself out." She slides the plate across the table, then takes my hands as I reach for it. "Hey, look at me." She gives me the soulful sisterly look we've shared since childhood. "This stuff with your father and Cruise doesn't change who you are."

I squeeze her hands and feel my eyes welling up. "You're the only sister I've ever had. The only sibling I want."

"Old Sicilian saying: members of a family often grow up under different roofs."

"Is that sorta like *you can pick your friends, but you can't pick your family*?"

"Something like that. Just because you have a blood relative doesn't mean you have to love that person. Or even like them. Hell, we've got an entire flock of black sheep in my family. And if you do have a half-sibling, no one says you have to accept this other person. If we can even find out who it is. And so what if your father knocked up another woman? It doesn't change your views of him. It's actually par for the course if you ask me."

"Rox, I'm more concerned with my mom. She went through enough this spring... and now this."

"Hey, he left seventeen years ago and she did fine. She's a survivor. Tougher than you think despite the outward emotions."

"Yeah, I know."

"You gonna tell her?"

"Not if I don't have to. It would hurt her too much and, honestly, what's the point? But I have to tell Sebastien because of the implications. Like Fuzzball said, a child from those two could have powers that are off the charts."

"Or this person might not have powers at all. The muses in my family skip a generation."

"That would be nice, but the way our luck runs there's another evil comic book villain out there."

"But suppose we find this person, Jillian, and he or she turns out to be a decent human being? Might be an incredible ally."

"With those two parents? I highly doubt it."

"Your father is the antichrist and you turned out okay. Evil can skip a generation as well. Or maybe good is a dominant gene."

"That's a nice way to look at it. I sure hope you're right." I look back at the pastry and lick my lips, my anxiety already having burned through the first one. "Can I have my cannoli now?"

She smiles and lets go of my hands. "Sure. I'll lend you a pair of my stretch pants."

"Smart ass."

"Just trying to lighten you up. Speaking of which, why don't you go spend some time with Ryan tonight?"

I look at the clock on the wall. "It's kinda late. And I don't wanna ride the subway at night."

"I didn't imply that you should. Just beam yourself over there. Jillian to Enterprise: energize."

I hear my mother sawing wood through her closed bedroom door as I make my way up the stairs to my own room. I'm mentally exhausted from all I've learned today and want to simply shut my brain off for a while. I close the door, take out my cell and text Ryan.

Are you still up? Desperate redhead ready to drop by.

I hit the send button and hear the familiar swoosh which tells me the message has been sent. Now I wait. I curl up in a ball, knees to my chest, and wrap my arms around my legs. I really don't want to be alone right now. Roxanne put things in perspective and made me feel a little better, as did my cannoli binge, but I need my boyfriend.

My phone dings and I eagerly hit the button that will reveal the message.

Sure, but take a cab. Don't want u on subway.

The hell with that. I stretch out on my bed, close my eyes, focus on his dorm room.

And materialize in front of him.

He jumps back, grabbing his chest. "Dammit, Sparks, you gotta warn me when you're gonna do that. It scares the hell out of me when you just appear."

"Sorry, I didn't want to wait."

"But I'm glad you're here. This is a nice surprise."

I move forward and wrap my arms around him, lean my head against his chest. He rubs his hands across my back, then pulls away and tilts my head up with one hand. "What's wrong, Sparks? You look like you've seen a ghost."

"You're not too far off."

I unload everything, telling him the story of my trip to Cruise's house, the photo, not telling mom. How my mind has been going off on tangents as I try to process the possibility that I have a half sibling out there somewhere. While wondering if that person is as evil as the parents. Or maybe someone who might possibly help us?

He kisses me on the top of the head and gently strokes my hair. "I'm sorry, Sparks. That's an awful lot to process. I don't know what to say."

"Don't say anything. Just hold me."

"That I can do."

He hugs me tight as I bury my head in his chest, breathing in his cologne. I really don't want to leave. "Ryan... can I stay here tonight?"

He pulls back and looks at me, eyes wide. "Seriously?"

"I don't mean... *that*. I mean spend the night. Sleeping here. With you just holding me."

"Your mother know you're here?"

"Doesn't matter. She trusts me. And we're not going to do anything."

"Sure. Besides, when we do take the big leap I want the real you. Physically, I mean."

"Yeah, me too."

Ryan gets into bed, still wearing a tee shirt and sweatpants, and I slide in next to him. I'm exhausted. I throw one leg over him while resting my head on his chest. "Sweet dreams, Sparks." He gently kisses my head.

"Not a problem anymore."

"Really?"

"Yeah. The angel's little trick with the ring works great. When I run into someone I don't like, I basically tell them to go away, snap my fingers and they disappear."

"Good. Glad to hear she can't screw with your head anymore."

I tilt my head to look at him. "Speaking of which, young man, in the dream she created the other night you were on the beach with some cheap stacked blonde in a string bikini who was all over you."

He leans his head up to look at me. "Really? Was she hot?"

I playfully slap him on the shoulder. "Watch it, Mister. I can beam outta here in a flash."

"I'm sure she was a slut. Thankfully I'm not into that type. Y'know. Cheap stacked blondes in bikinis. Don't even care to look at 'em."

"You really are mastering the care and feeding of redheads."

He leans back, rests his head on the pillow and wraps an arm around me.

I've never felt better as I fall asleep.

Chapter 10

When I first woke up I was disappointed I did so in my own bed. When I got up to look in the mirror, I was glad I did.

The last thing the man of my dreams needs to see before we take the big leap is how I look in the morning. Not that I'm a candidate for the road company of *Tales from the Crypt* or anything, but my combed-by-an-eggbeater hair, droopy eyes and dragon breath aren't exactly a man's idea of a fantasy. I'd personally like to do what Kristin Wiig did at the beginning of *Bridesmaids*: wake up before the guy does, get gussied up, go back to bed and pretend to be asleep. Then when he wakes up I'll look as good as I did when I turned in and he'll think I'm radiant 24/7. Of course, after we're married there'll be no turning back for Ryan from this haggard ball and chain.

Still, it was wonderful falling asleep in his arms, feeling safe and protected. I've never had such a restful night. Even had a nice dream that wasn't a product of someone's attempt to break us up.

Anyway, that's the least of our concerns on this Saturday evening, which does not have me dressed to the nines for a night on the town. Once again our date night gets blown up by the forces of evil. Ryan and I are at The Summit waiting for some evil minion of my father to contact him. Sebastien has come up with a terrific plan. My father's brain waves are being closely monitored, and as soon as he exhibits a change similar to the last time he was contacted, Ryan will zip into his mind and hopefully unlock a few secrets and answer some questions.

And maybe find out who's contacting him.

Speaking of which, Sebastien has had his geek squad pouring through the massive amount of information I copied from Cruise's laptop. We're seated around a round table covered with stacks of papers that have been printed out. "What you sent has been invaluable," he says.

"Have you gone through it all?"

"No, we're perhaps halfway through. But it contains a great deal of information about your father and his network of followers."

"Did you get names?"

"Unfortunately, Cruise was careful. And she's using code names for your father's plan. All biblical terms. Jericho, Babel, names like that. It appears she is associated with Babylon."

"My, how appropriate."

Sebastien takes out a single sheet. "Your father apparently had a three part plan, and had designated one person to oversee each part." He takes a deep breath and pauses for a few moments.

"What, Sebastien?" I ask.

"As I said, there are three parts of his plan. Babel was the first, which thankfully we defeated. To be followed by Babylon and Jericho. We surmise that Cruise is overseeing the Babylon portion of the plan." He stops and looks to the side for a moment, then down at the paper.

"What aren't you telling me, Sebastien?"

"The one real name on the chart is under Jericho. It is the person your father obviously wanted to oversee the implementation of part three. The endgame." He slides the paper toward me and Ryan.

My hair stands on end as I see my own name.

Ryan wraps an arm around me. "Calm down, Sparks. It's just your father's warped way of thinking."

Sebastien nods. "This document is time stamped right before

you took down your father, right after you let him think you were on board. Remember, he wanted you to be the liaison for the cell phone, to be the face of the company for your generation. He obviously wanted you to be the point person for the final part of the plan."

"Sorry, it just creeps me out," I say.

Sebastien hands us another sheet. "Here's a flow chart showing who is in charge of what. Apparently, your father had assembled three teams to work under the three leaders. Of course, we don't know if one team leader knew what the other was working on, or what may have changed since he became incapacitated."

"How many people are we talking here?" asks Ryan.

"Maybe two dozen. But there are no names, simply titles."

I scan the sheet, but the notations make no sense. It's all code. "Cruise has to be one of the other two team leaders."

"Yes. It makes sense that he would have a dream weaver as one of his key subordinates."

"I wonder if there's a power struggle with her and whoever is the other team leader," says Ryan.

"Definitely something to consider," says Sebastien. "But I would guess she might have the upper hand, considering her powers and her, uh, relationship with your father." Sebastien's eyes grow sad. "I'm sorry, Jillian, I know that was a difficult discovery for you to make."

"Nothing surprises me about the man anymore." I look through the window at his comatose body, which has begun to look fragile and pale. A far cry from the powerful man who almost took down society a few months ago. "He obviously didn't give a damn about anyone but himself. He certainly didn't care about me or my mother."

Ryan sees my eyes welling up, reaches under the table, takes my hand, and entwines his fingers with mine.

He doesn't even need to read my mind anymore to know what I'm thinking.

"There's a little more of great importance," says Sebastien.

I shake my head. "Not sure I can take much more, but bring it on."

He hands me the paper. "It's a correspondence between Cruise and someone else in the organization. But we don't know the identity of the recipient."

I read the simple email:

Jillian's dream implantation and brain wave alteration complete. Though her bond with Ryan is a strong one, creating doubt in her mind through the use of physical and mental temptation should be effective. She is still an innocent teenager in her first serious relationship and should be very susceptible to physical stimuli. Both real life and dream interactions will be very effective in making her have second thoughts about her current relationship.

Jake will not be a problem as he is already entranced, and I should have the little telekinetic under control at the proper time. Driving him and his girlfriend apart will significantly weaken Roxanne, who is basically ruled by her emotions and should easily be taken.

The last line of the email gives me chills. "Oh my God, she's planning to kill Roxanne."

"We'll protect her," says Sebastien. "And you've already foiled her plan to drive them apart."

I bite my lower lip and am close to tears. "But she killed a muse!"

"I won't let anything bad happen to her," says Ryan, pulling me close. "They've thrown everything they've got at us and haven't been able to break any of us apart, Sparks. We defeated your father, and no one was as powerful as he was. We're unbeatable as a team, you know that."

"God, I hope so. But her anger towards us might be a factor.

We may have put the man she loved out of commission. She may simply want to get even."

Two hours later Sebastien, Ryan and I are still pouring through the mass of printouts from Cruise's computer. I've seen everything from term papers to a class syllabus to a bunch of stuff that doesn't make sense and is obviously in code. The latter get put into a pile, since we're assuming those pages hold the keys to the answers we seek. A technician in a white lab coat reads a magazine as he sits next to the machine that is monitoring my father's brain waves.

And when the machine beeps, we all sit up straight.

The technician leans closer to the monitor, then turns to Sebastien. "It's happening, Sir. Contact is being made right now."

Ryan gets up and quickly moves close to my father's chamber. "I'm on it." He closes his eyes, puts his hand on the side of the steel chamber and the machine beeps again.

"Ryan is in," says the technician.

Sebastien and I both get up and take positions behind the technician as Ryan remains quiet with his eyes closed. I'm within a couple of feet if anything goes wrong, but his face remains calm and peaceful.

"Separating all three patterns," says the technician, who punches a few buttons. The screen divides horizontally into thirds. My father's name appears above the top brain wave pattern, Ryan's above the one in the middle, and a question mark tops the lower third. "Copying that of the visitor."

"Anything you see out of the ordinary regarding our mystery guest?" I ask.

"Heightened activity in the Delta waves." He points to my father's pattern. "He's showing significant changes. He's being accessed."

I look at Ryan's pattern, wanting to make sure it doesn't change. "Anything happening with Ryan?"

The tech shakes his head. "He's fine. No changes."

Suddenly my father's waves jump violently up and down,

looking like a seismograph during a major earthquake. I catch some movement out of the corner of my eye, look up.

And see my father moving.

His fingers twitch. "Look! Is he waking up?"

The tech shakes his head. "No. His entire brain is being accessed now. It's natural that there should be some physical activity. It's a simple neural response."

My father's arms and legs begin to shake. He looks like he's having some sort of a seizure. His brain wave patterns and those of the visitor are both jerking up and down, while Ryan's remain on an even keel. His face is still calm.

And then the visitor's brain waves disappear. My father's go back to normal, he stops twitching.

Ryan opens his eyes. "Wow. That was intense."

"Do you know who it was?" I ask.

He shakes his head. "No idea. I couldn't even tell the sex of the person. But it's someone your father knows extremely well."

"Both brains showed significant activity," says Sebastien. "Could you access what was being done?"

Ryan nods. "Yeah. And you're not gonna like it."

My pulse spikes. "My father's not getting his powers back, is he?"

"No, he's still powerless. But the person who made contact basically copied his brain."

Sebastien originally planned to bring Roxanne to The Summit to discuss the incident of Ms. Cruise killing the muse. But when he saw how upset I was and knew I would tell her about the email, he decided I would be a better person to go over it with her. I'm surprised he would delegate something like this to me, but he seems confident this is the way to go. Especially since Cruise thinks Roxanne's emotions can be used against her. Honestly, I don't disagree. Her short fuse is easily lit.

Rox hops up the steps to our front porch on this beautiful Sunday afternoon and joins me on the wicker bench. "How was the trip?"

"The visitor showed up on schedule. We don't know who it is, but my father's brain was copied."

"Copied?"

"The experts aren't sure how it was done, but Ryan knows it happened."

"So... what does this mean?"

"We're not sure. He doesn't have powers anymore, but his subconscious might have information about his master plan that was never shared with anyone else."

I go over the flow charts and other information Sebastien shared from Cruise's computer. Then I pull out the single sheet of paper that contains the email. "Okay, I want you to remain calm when I show you this."

She furrows her brow. "Why? Is this something that will make me upset?"

"That's putting it mildly."

I hand her the paper and study her face as she reads it. Her eyes narrow, her jaw clenches and her hands ball into fists. She finishes reading and tosses it on the bench. "Bitch."

"Let me guess. That Sicilian revenge chromosome has just shifted into high gear."

"I'll kick her ass."

"This is exactly the reaction she wants from you, which is why I'm sharing it with you now. When and if you two have this muse-siren steel cage smackdown, I want you to be in control of your emotions."

"Are you implying I'm emotional?"

"I'm not implying anything. It's a stone cold fact. You will need to remain calm."

She rolls her eyes. "Jillian, you think that's even possible with me?"

"Honestly, no, but I want you to be aware of it. She's planning to use that hot head of yours against you."

"I'll crush that skinny bitch like a grape."

"Rox, I know damn well you could kick her ass, but if there is a battle, it won't be physical. We're talking her power against yours."

She exhales deeply and looks away. "Damn it, Jillian, why do you always have to make sense?"

"That's why we're such a good team. We know how to protect each other. Now, do you think you're calm enough to hear about the incident?"

Her eyes fill with sadness. "You mean how she killed the muse?"

"Yeah. We can do this later if you want."

"No, get it over with."

"Okay. It's actually a very short story. Cruise made an appointment with a muse, acting as a normal client looking for inspiration. When the muse went into her head, she attacked her on a subconscious level. The muse ended up in a coma and eventually died."

"So it wasn't a singing contest like the legend."

"No. And the muse had no idea she was going to be attacked."

Roxanne nods. "Then we have the advantage."

"How's that?"

"Well, if the only way for a siren to kill a muse is for a muse to get into her head, then I simply don't go into her head."

"You forget the dream weaver aspect of this. She could make you think you're dreaming and make you do a session with her."

"Oh. Hadn't thought of that."

I take her hand and squeeze it. "We'll figure it out, Rox."

"Maybe so. Or maybe we reverse the process and take the fight to her."

Chapter 11

My cell phone brings a smile as I see Ryan is calling. "Hey."

"Sparks, turn on channel seven."

I hang up my jacket and move to the living room. "Why, what's going on?"

"Just turn it on and call me back later."

He hangs up. I grab the remote and fire it at the television. The picture clears and I see a split screen of an anchor-babe on one side and an empty podium on the other, with Rebecca Cruise walking up to it.

"This is a ground breaking piece of legislation," says the anchor, "if she can get it passed."

"Hey, Mom!" I yell. "Come watch this! Hurry up!"

Mom comes running in, licking chocolate batter off a wooden spoon as she goes. "What's so important?" I point at the TV, she looks at it and glares. "Oh. *Her*."

The split screen cuts to a shot of Cruise moving to the podium, with a half dozen other senators behind her. A horde of reporters are waiting. There's an easel covered by a red sheet next to the podium. "Thank you all for coming," she says, flashing her warm smile. "Today I, along with the members of the United States Senate who have joined me, are announcing that we will introduce a bi-partisan bill that will end identity theft as we know it. We are proposing the creation of a national identity card which will be issued to every man, woman and child in the United States. While this may sound like a massive project, and it is, in the long run it will make all of our lives better and protect our personal assets. Once we have every person in the database Americans will be much safer from criminals who profit from identity theft. In addition, this will also eliminate voter fraud."

"Stop identity theft, my ass," says Mom. "She's about to *steal* everyone's identity. And then do God knows what with it."

Cruise pulls the sheet covering the easel and unveils it, which features a sample giant ID card with a photo, name, and fingerprint. "This is what everyone will be issued should this legislation pass. It will entail a massive campaign to get everyone registered." She takes a pointer and taps the fingerprint. "You'll notice that each card will carry the fingerprint of the person it is issued to, so no one will ever be able to do anything should you lose your card or have it stolen. Each card is unique to you and you alone, as unique as your fingerprints. It cannot be duplicated. It will be your personal assurance that your identity is protected."

"She's picking up where the cell phone left off," I say.

"Or maybe this was phase two of the plan," says Mom.

A male reporter fires a question. "Doesn't this infringe on people's privacy?"

She smiled and hummed a bit. The reporter's face relaxed. "It's no different than a driver's license, when you think about it. And at some point everyone needs proper identification. You'll be able to swipe this like a credit card when someone asks for ID. And your fingerprint will verify that you really are the person on the card."

Mom shakes her head. "She just did her siren number on that guy. Watch, the only tough questions will come from women."

Sure enough, mom is right, as the male reporters lob softballs which Cruise easily knocks out of the park. She deftly side-steps a few hard questions from the female reporters, and it's clear she's in charge of the room. She announces the bill will be brought to the floor in a day or two for debate, asks for the public to contact their local member of Congress to support it, then wraps things up.

I hit the mute button before the anchor-babe has a chance to speak. "So, waddaya think?"

"It's bigger than the phone," says Mom, sitting on the couch. "Not everyone had one of your father's phones. But everyone will have one of these. And the law will require it."

"What's the deal with the fingerprint?"

"It's gotta be her way of being connected to everyone. Trust me, they'll be taking more than a fingerprint when they issue these things."

"You think this is connected to someone copying my father's brain?"

"Has to be. But how they're going to use it is anyone's guess."

Mom gets back up and heads to the kitchen to finish baking whatever chocolate concoction she's got going. I follow for two reasons: I want to talk to her about my father and I traditionally lick the bowl.

She adds chopped walnuts to what I recognize as dark chocolate brownie mix. "You're making Ghirardellis?"

"Your favorite."

"Yours too." She mixes the nuts into the batter, then starts spooning it out into a prepared glass pan.

"Whoa! Not all of it."

She leaves a significant amount of batter in the bowl, then hands it to me with a spatula. "I know what my little girl needs." She runs a finger across the side of the bowl, scooping up a bit of batter, then licks it. "Tribute."

I fill up the spatula with the rich chocolate batter and lick it clean, the rich cocoa giving me the familiar sugar rush. "Oh yeah."

"Needed a fix, huh?"

"You know me too well, Mom." She puts the brownies in the oven and sets the timer. "Hey, can I ask you something personal?"

"No, I don't wanna get fixed up on a date. There's no way I'm going on one of those Internet sites for middle-aged singles."

"Not that, though I wouldn't mind seeing you with someone if that's what's holding you back. You sacrificed enough for me."

"That's sweet of you, Jillian, but not right now. Maybe someday when we're done saving the world. So what did you wanna ask me?"

I pause a moment, thinking about how to phrase what I want to say, since I know this is a touchy subject. "It's about my father. Do you, you know, still think about him? The way he was... the way he probably is now... at The Summit?"

She sits down across from me and steals another finger full of batter. "I'd be lying if I said I didn't. Seeing him again after all these years... it did bring back a lot of memories I thought I'd buried. Sometimes I wonder how much of the original man I fell in love with is left. If the guy I fell in love with is still there."

"Mom, if you want, I could—"

"Hell, no! You're not healing him."

"I just—"

"Don't bring it up again, Jillian. There's too much risk."

She looks down at the table and wipes a tear from her eye, a reminder of exactly how much she's sacrificed for me.

And how she continues to do it.

Halloween couldn't have come at a better time. We all need a night of fun and chocolate, to go to an adult costume party where anything goes and a sugar high is inevitable. And since I wanted to let my hair down, I needed something revealing to get out of my comfort zone.

I considered going as a sexy version of Dorothy from The Wizard of Oz, which is a good costume for a redhead, but given the fact that I have the power to "beam" myself anywhere, I've gone with a little inside joke and chosen a vintage Star Trek uniform. You know, the one from the original series with the hemline up to the ass and some go-go boots. Ryan's jaw dropped when he saw me. He said, "Resistance is futile," and even though that was from the wrong series (Captain Kirk never encountered the Borg, though he would have kicked their ass) I appreciated the compliment. I pointed my toy tricorder at him, told him his heart rate was up and that he would need intensive care later in sick bay.

Once Roxanne found out I had ruled out Dorothy, she snatched the idea right up and went to work with a needle and thread, taking the hem on a gingham dress way, way up. She carried a stuffed dog, but with her incredibly long legs in platform ruby heels, no one was paying any attention to Toto. (Jake took one look at her and said, "There really *is* no place like home.") It's kinda funny having a Dorothy with a New York accent and attitude. "Fuhgeddaboudit. I got your flyin' monkeys *right here*."

Rox and I are headed back to our table from the ladies room when she stops dead in her tracks and her jaw drops. "Oh. My. God."

I look around to find out what has gotten this reaction and don't see anything out of the ordinary. "What?"

She cocks her head in the direction of the refreshment table. "Perfect ten at nine o'clock. Your, uh, dream guy just arrived. In a very nice costume. Yowza."

I look to my left and see Trip dressed as a Chippendale dancer. Black spandex pants, a collar and cuffs. That's it. My eyes bug out, as the sight of his shirtless body in real life is even more impressive than what I saw in my dream. "Damn."

"You mean *hot* damn. Geez, he's gotta be twice as big as Jake. Look at the size of his chest. And those abs. His muscles have muscles." Rox licks her lips. "I want."

"You're taken."

She shrugs, her eyes locked on Trip. "Wanting and having are two different things, my friend. I can want something even though I can't have it. I want a Rolls Royce but I know I can't have it. And that boy is a fully loaded Rolls. But damn, I want."

"Take a number," I say, as I see every girl in the room looking in his direction. Aspen, who is dressed as a cave girl, must also notice this as she moves closer and wraps an arm around his waist. She's nearly six feet tall but looks petite next to Trip. "He's already taken as well. Note the tall supermodel doubling as a clinging vine."

She wrinkles her nose. "It's always a stacked, leggy blonde, isn't it?"

"This coming from a stacked, leggy brunette. But Aspen's really nice. And funny. You'd like her."

"I'd like to *be* her right now."

Suddenly, we're back in high school. "Why, what would you do to him?"

"It's more like what he could do to me. He's big enough to carry me away, which doesn't happen often for a girl my size." She turns to me and raises one eyebrow. "Of course, *you've* already had that pleasure. I assume you enjoyed the ride?"

The image of Trip carrying me to the infirmary with my sprained ankle flashes through my brain and makes me blush. "It, uh, wasn't exactly unpleasant."

"Yeah, right. To quote yourself, you're taken."

"True." I can't stop staring as Trip gets a couple of drinks and hands one to Aspen, who is busy running her hands over his chest.

"Though from your look it appears you've still got it bad for the guy."

"I'm trying not to think about it, Rox."

"I'm not having that problem. And if you're trying not to think about it, stop staring at him like he's dinner and you're a starving woman. Or I'll have to get you a drool cup."

I finally break out of my trance and turn to her. "Fine. And since you're obviously stuck on the *size matters* subject, may I remind you that Jake proves good things come in small packages."

"Very true. But you know serious eye candy does that to me. I just had a superficial cheap slut moment. I'm dressed like one, so I'm simply acting the part."

"Right. I was beginning to worry you might be obsessing about the fact Jake is so much shorter than you."

"You kidding? I love having a boyfriend who's portable. If we ever get married I'll be carrying him over the threshold. He lets me embrace my inner Amazon." We start walking back to our table. "You know, it might be good if Ryan saw that," she says, pointing at Trip.

"Are you out of your mind? He's already intimidated. The last thing he needs is a view of the guy without a shirt."

"I meant seeing Trip with a hot blonde draped all over him."

"Oh."

"Might help with the jealousy problem, ya think? If he saw those two he might not consider Trip a threat anymore."

"You've got a point." Meanwhile, what do we do about *my* jealousy problem? I feel the green-eyed monster rearing its ugly head as my eyes lock one more time on the best-looking man I've ever seen.

We get back to the table where Ryan and Jake are busy eating. Ryan's looking hot dressed as a football player, complete with eye black. Jake is cute as hell in his genie costume. I note that Trip and Aspen are now doing a slow dance in the middle of the floor.

Roxanne taps Jake on the shoulder, whispers in his ear and he nods. He nudges Ryan in the arm, then points to the dance floor. "Dude, don't think you have to worry about someone going after your girl. Those two look like they need to get a room."

I notice Ryan begin to smile as he sees Aspen hanging all over Trip. "Yeah, no kidding," he says.

I reach under the table and pat Roxanne on the leg. She turns to me and winks, then leans over to whisper in my ear. "You're welcome. But I still want."

Yeah. Me too.

I find myself in a massive modern kitchen filled with stainless steel appliances. A large black granite center island sits in the middle underneath a rack of copper saucepans. A large simmering pot which looks and smells like my mother's beef stew is on the gas cook top, while the aroma of baking cookies blends in from the oven. I'm dressed in an outfit much too nice for the kitchen, an eggshell silk blouse and gray wool skirt with conservative pumps.

And a look at my hand reveals Carrielle's emerald ring.

So my dream has landed me in a McMansion. Hey, I coulda landed in a trailer park so I won't complain.

But is this my dream or one provided by the dream weaver? Inquiring minds wanna know.

My heels click on the black and white marble floor as I walk around the kitchen. (Seriously, who wears heels to cook?) A peek into the living room shows off beautiful red leather furniture and massive oak antiques atop gleaming dark hardwood floors. A look out one kitchen window reveals a large swimming pool in the center of a manicured back yard, while another window frames a gleaming red Mercedes convertible in the driveway with a vanity license plate that has my name on it. Okay, so I'm rich in this dream. I could get used to this in real life.

I hear the front door open, followed by a chorus of, "Mom, we're home!"

Mom? Me?

I hear footsteps, then see the source, as a boy and girl around eight or nine years old run into the kitchen and wrap their arms around my waist, one on each side of me. "Hey there," I say, not knowing what to do. I study their faces as they look up and smile at me. The little girl is slender with red hair, freckles and eyes that match mine, both in color and a devilish look. She's a definite Mini-Me. The little boy has neatly parted dark hair and looks sharp in a school uniform, dark slacks and a blue button down oxford shirt. I can already tell he's gonna be a heart breaker. "Uh... how was school?"

"Great, Mom," says the girl.

The boy reaches into his back pocket and thrusts out a blue folder. "Report card day!" The girl then hands me hers.

I open them and see a parade of A's. Cool, my kids take after me. I look at the tops of the cards and see the boy's name is Scott, the girl's Roxanne. The fact I named my daughter after my best friend makes me smile. "Wow, terrific report cards, guys! I'm proud of you!"

I hear the door open again, which makes the kids whip their heads in that direction. "Daddy's home!" says the girl, as they run to greet him.

I can't help but feel warm inside at the fairy tale dream as I wait for Ryan, but it fades when my "husband" walks into the kitchen.

Trip Logan.

He's decked out in a dark gray windowpane business suit, white shirt and red striped tie and smiles as he sees me. "Hey, babe," he says, moving toward me.

I shake my head and put out my hand, giving him the Heisman. "Whoa, you're outta here," I say, and snap my fingers.

Nothing happens.

"What are you talking about?" he asks, as he reaches out for me with both hands.

I back up. "Go, get out! Now!" I snap my fingers again but nothing happens.

Both children look puzzled. "Mom, what's wrong?" asks the boy.

Trip's smile fades as he furrows his brow. "Jillian, why are you acting so upset?"

"I'm supposed to be able to control my dreams and I know this is a dream. I want you gone. So get lost." I snap my fingers again.

He smiles and shakes his head. "That's funny. Control your dreams. You can't control your dreams."

"Sure I can. But for some reason I can't control this one."

"You don't get it, do you?"

"Get what?"

“This isn’t your dream, Jillian. It’s mine.”

Chapter 12

My heart rate spikes as my eyes widen in fear. "What the hell?"

"I'm not kidding. This is *my* dream," Trip says casually. "That's all. You happen to be in it. Jillian, it's nothing to be afraid of." He waves his arms around the kitchen "None of this is real."

"Fine, then I'm leaving," I say, as I walk around the island to avoid him. I leave the kitchen and head toward the front door.

Which is no longer there.

"What happened to the door?"

Trip follows, moves in front of me and smiles as he puts his hands on my shoulders, sending electricity through my body. "It's my dream, Jillian. I want you to stay. Please don't be upset with me."

I twist my body away and back up. A quick look for another escape reveals that all the doors and windows are now solid walls. "I don't want to stay, Trip. Let me go. Please."

"You can't leave because this isn't real and it's my dream. There's no harm done. Let's just sit and talk." He gestures toward the dining room table.

"No. You know damn well you want to do more than talk." I close my eyes and focus. "Wake up, Jillian. Dammit, wake up!"

Nothing happens.

I open my eyes and see him sitting at the head of the table. He pats the chair next to him. "C'mon. Sit and talk awhile. Really,

Jillian, I just like being around you. In this dream we must be a happy married couple with a couple of cute kids, that's all."

What the hell, I'm obviously stuck. The damn dream weaver has figured out that if I can control my own dreams she's going to send me into someone else's. May as well try to get some information while I'm here. "Fine. But just *talk*. Keep your hands to yourself."

He folds his hands on the table. "Fair enough. I just want to spend some time with you."

I walk through the living room, pausing a bit to take in the photo grouping on one wall. A wedding photo with me looking radiant in a gown while Trip would give James Bond a run for his money in a tux. Several photos of the children, all of us on various vacations. The two of us on a beach, my arms wrapped around his waist. A family portrait that includes my Mom, who is beaming as she sits between her grandchildren. I move to the table and take a seat. "Trip, do you know why this is happening? Why I'm in your dream?"

"I'm assuming because this is what I daydream almost every day. I guess it finally manifested itself in a real dream. I recently read a book on lucid dreaming and this is called dream incubation. If you focus on what you want to dream about, sometimes it happens. This is what I was thinking about before I fell asleep so it carried over into this dream."

"You daydream this? Me and you with two kids in a mansion?"

He blushes as he nods. "Happily ever after. I know, Jillian, it's corny and a little embarrassing. I realize you're taken and have a serious boyfriend, but I can't help imagining what things would be like if you were available."

I furrow my brow. "Trip, you're dating a terrific girl. Aspen's fun, smart and a helluva lot prettier than me. Why don't you daydream about her? I thought you liked her a lot."

"I do. She's a great girl and we have fun together. She's in bed with me right now."

My eyes widen. "Wow, Trip, what a great pickup line. Even for a dream. Great way to win a girl's heart."

"Haven't you ever had a fantasy, Jillian? Pretended you were with someone else when you were with your boyfriend?"

My face tightens. "No. When I'm with Ryan he's all I think about. Because he's all I want."

He shrugs. "Well, we're different, that's all. Guys are different, especially when it comes to women we can't have. I couldn't get you out of my head after seeing you at the party tonight. You looked hot in that Star Trek uniform. Damn, you've got great legs."

"In case you haven't noticed, Aspen is built like a supermodel. Most guys would kill for a girl like that. And since she's in your bed right now, it should be obvious she's crazy about you. Why don't you wake up and play around with her? It will actually be real."

"I'm sorry, Jillian, but I'm intoxicated with *you*. I simply like to imagine what it would be like if you weren't attached. I know you're attracted to me. I was hoping to catch your eye at the party with my costume."

"I think you caught every girl's eye dressing up as a male stripper."

"So, you liked what you saw?"

Hell yeah, but I'm not telling him that. "Trip, this conversation isn't helping things. I am off the market, for good. Ryan and I are getting married some day. I love him, he loves me, we're soul mates, end of story. And I think this is also the end of our discussion."

"Will you at least admit you're attracted to me?"

"Trip, you said you wanted to sit and talk, and we've done that. For whatever reason you've got the hots for me while you've got Aspen in your bed. That's your problem, not mine. Please let me go."

He shrugs and exhales as he looks down. "I guess I can't force you to love me, but it's a nice fantasy. I'm sorry if I've offended you." I can see his eyes growing moist.

I dial down my anger a notch as it's clear he's hurt. "Look, Trip, you're a nice guy but you should know you're being manipulated.

And so am I. You might find this hard to believe, but there's this woman called a dream weaver who's main objective is to drive me and Ryan apart and she's using you to do it. You're not really into me, you're being made to believe it. I'm actually a mystic seer and I did a reading for Aspen and saw you two falling in love. If you're not there already."

"Wow, this dream is getting weird. But I guess that's typical since we're not dealing with reality."

I get up, turn and see the front door is still not there. I fold my arms and glare at him. "Dammit, Trip let me go. Open the door."

"Tell you what. One kiss and you can go."

I roll my eyes. "Oh, for goodness sake—"

"It's a dream, Jillian. One kiss. Harmless."

"I already kissed you in real life. And that was anything but harmless."

He smiles and points to his cheek.

The front door still isn't there.

I shake my head and throw up my hands. "Fine. If it's the only way out of here."

I move toward Trip, lean down and kiss him.

And then I can't stop.

I now know what women mean when they use the term "walk of shame."

No, things didn't get *that* far. But if my alarm clock hadn't jolted me out of Trip's dream, who knows what might have happened. Still, I'm horribly ashamed of myself, even if none of it was real. Ashamed that I "cheated" on Ryan even if it wasn't real. Ashamed that I didn't want it to stop, that I enjoyed the hell out of it. Ashamed that I rationalized it by repeatedly telling myself, "No big deal, it's only a dream. Ryan will never know."

I thought I was out of there with one peck on the cheek. But as I leaned in he turned his head so our lips would meet.

It was like the kiss magnetized my entire body, connected me to him in a manner that wouldn't let me leave. I was powerless as I attacked him with a hunger I've never known, one even stronger than the first time we connected. He pulled me onto his lap and my body molded itself into his like it was a perfect fit. The physical chemistry was incredible, nothing even close to what I feel with Ryan. We made out for what seemed like an hour even though time has no meaning in dreams. I'd ripped open his shirt so hard the buttons flew across the floor and was busy running my hands over his incredible chest and shoulders while I straddled him, kissing Trip like I was trying to devour him. I was totally in control of him. His hands gently slipped under my blouse, beginning to explore. His touch only heightening my attraction. I didn't want it to ever end.

And when the alarm woke me up, I was actually upset I'd been interrupted.

The tears are already flowing as I make my way downstairs despite the fact I'm in serious need of a cold shower. I hear the coffee pot gurgling and know Mom is already up, so I pick up the pace. She glances up from the morning paper, takes one look at my face and immediately gets up with her arms outstretched.

I run to her, hug her hard as she wraps her arms around me. I rest my head on her shoulder and my emotions explode.

"Good God, Jillian, what's wrong?"

I'm sobbing now, tears streaming down my face. "My dream. The dream weaver...and I cheated..."

She takes my head and pulls back to look at me. "I thought that emerald ring thing solved that problem."

"It wasn't my dream, Mom. She sent me into someone else's dream. I couldn't get out. I was trapped."

"Whose dream?"

"Trip Logan's."

Mom's eyes narrow into the death stare. "We've gotta take that bitch out. I'm tired of her messing with my little girl. This is getting out of hand." She brushes my hair back and takes my hands. "You say you were in someone else's dream?"

"Yeah. I thought it was a nice dream when it started out and when I found out it belonged to Trip, I couldn't escape. We were in this house and all the doors and windows disappeared. If the alarm hadn't gone off I might have been in there even longer."

"Wow. Being able to send you into someone else's dream is not part of the legend." She reaches up and wipes my tears. "It's okay, sweetie. Still just a dream. What did you mean when you say you cheated?"

The tears start again, she sits me down and places a box of tissues in front of me. The coffee machine beeps, she fixes two cups, slides a chair next to me and wraps an arm around my shoulders as she sits down. I tell her the whole story, sobbing the entire time, feeling like I have lost control.

"Okay," she says. "First, you didn't cheat on Ryan. All of this... stuff going on in your head... isn't real."

I stare at my coffee as I wrap both hands around the cup. "Mom, I didn't want to leave. I knew it was wrong but I kept..."

"Did it ever occur to you that she's doing the same thing to Trip?"

Her words make me stop and think for a moment. It makes sense. A guy who looks like that with an off the charts gorgeous girlfriend... is obsessed with *me*? "I never considered it."

"Well, consider it. You saw him and his girlfriend in a reading, right?"

"Yeah. It looked like they were in love. No, I'm sure of it."

"There ya go. She's screwin' with *his* mind too, kiddo. He's in love with the other girl. The dream weaver is still using him to make you question your relationship with Ryan."

I nod slightly. "It makes sense. But I'm still confused about my feelings for Trip. I mean, we have such incredible physical chemistry and he does things to me Ryan never has. I wanted him, Mom. I wanted him bad. I've never felt that about Ryan. Not like that anyway. I kept telling myself it was only a dream but I didn't stop. I *couldn't* stop." I feel the tears coming and my voice cracks. "And

I hate to say this, but I think I want him in real life."

"Oh, don't be ridiculous. Look, I have a naughty dream every once in a while, you know. I don't even wanna tell you what I did to Christian Bale last week."

I can't help but laugh at her attempt to lighten the mood. The tears slow down as I wipe my eyes. "Thought you were hot for Bradley Cooper?"

"Hey, this girl's not gonna be tied down to one guy. I need variety in my fantasies, you know?"

"So who else you got on your roster?"

"I've had a thing for Pierce Brosnan for a while. I fancy myself as Miss Moneypenny. Judi Dench is out of the office, and, you know... one thing leads to another."

"So that's why we have all his James Bond DVDs."

"Well, the VHS copies wore out."

"Mother!"

"Look, Jillian, this is simply a teenage fantasy for you. You just went from spending all day with high school boys as young as fourteen to being surrounded by college *men*. In case you forgot, you just turned eighteen. You're a kid in a sexy candy store and the best thing in it is on sale and wants to be in your shopping cart. Let me ask you this. How many guys in high school looked like Trip?"

"Are you kidding? None. There was no one even close. Actually, he may be the hottest guy I've ever met. Plus he's a real gentleman, he's smart, he's funny—"

"That's why she's throwing him at you. One big hunky piece of temptation. He's what your generation calls the total package." She smiles as she sips her coffee. "You know that old ratty New York Mets shirt you sleep in?"

"Yeah, what about it?"

"Why don't you throw it away?"

"Don't change the subject, Mom. I need you to help me figure this out. I have to get Trip outta my head."

"Indulge me for a minute. Why don't you toss the shirt?"

I roll my eyes. "Because it's the most comfortable thing I have to sleep in. I *love* that shirt."

She reaches out, takes my hands, squeezes them and looks into my soul. "Right. You *love* that shirt, holes, rips and all. It's the same with men. Once you get past the physical stuff and the sex, you have to feel comfortable with someone. There's always gonna be a guy who's better looking and seems like the perfect man who you'll be attracted to. But you already have that guy with Ryan. He may not compare physically with this guy, but you're very comfortable with him. And when you get older that's all that matters. That's what love really is."

The coffee cup slides onto my table and I look up into Aspen's glowing face. "Hey, matchmaker," she says, as she sits down.

"Hey yourself. I take it from your look that things are going well."

She beaming as she licks her lips. "It was a *very* happy Halloween last night. Let's say there were only treats and no tricks."

I smile and nod. Some good news about her relationship with Trip getting stronger could make me feel better. "Considering your costumes, I can only imagine what the treats were."

Her smile gets bigger. "Ah, you saw the huge Chippendale on my arm. The outfit was my idea."

"You clever little vixen. No spilled drink this time?"

"Honey, you can only use that trick once. And the shirt didn't exist."

"Makes sense."

"But, hey, I didn't invent the thing, so you're welcome to steal it. Consider it to be in the public domain."

"Thanks, I'll give it a shot. And I suppose since you were dressed like a cave girl he hit you on the head with his club and carried you away."

"What can I say? Yabba dabba do me."

The great line makes me laugh. Aspen is such a quick wit and so nice I'm glad things are going well for her. "So, I take it your *after party* went on for quite a while."

She raises both eyebrows. "We went to my place and played fistful of dollars."

My face tightened. "You dressed your boyfriend like a male stripper and you went home to watch a Clint Eastwood spaghetti western?"

"Duh-uh. Not the movie, silly! Trip was a Chippendale, I had a bunch of dollar bills. Do the math, girl!"

The image of Aspen tucking dollar bills into Trip's waistband flashes through my mind and makes me blush. "Sorry, sometimes I miss the obvious."

She takes a sip of coffee, leans forward and lowers her voice. "Anyway, he spent the night and it was terrific. Jillian, I don't usually kiss and tell but the guy is incredible."

"I wouldn't expect any less looking at him. And he's a really nice guy. You're a lucky girl. You two make a gorgeous couple."

"Thank you, though I must say it's a bit unnerving being with a guy who's better looking than me."

"You're not exactly chopped liver, Aspen. You could be a model and I saw plenty of guys checking you out last night."

"That part I'm used to. But being with a guy like Trip... I mean, women are constantly staring at him, and they don't even try to hide it."

Thankfully she doesn't have an accusing look for me despite the fact that I was locked on Trip like a heat seeking missile. "Yeah, some girls are so rude. Steal a glance, for goodness sake."

"I know. I went to the ladies room at one point and some girl was hitting on him when I came back."

"But he went home with *you*, that's the important thing."

"Very true. Speaking of which, after I thought I drained him last night, I wake up this morning and he's, you know," she looks around to make sure no one can hear, "needing to be serviced."

Really? Wonder how he got that way?

She adds a little sugar to her coffee and stirs it in. "Boy's got stamina, I'll give him that."

"Again, lucky you. And he's very fortunate to have a great girl."

She gives me a friendly pat on the shoulder. "Thanks to you! And speaking of lucky, I saw you at a table with a couple of hot guys last night. The cute little genie is yours?"

"Nope, that's Jake, and he belongs to my best friend Roxanne. She was dressed as Dorothy from the Wizard of Oz."

"The Amazon with the legs up to her neck?"

"That's her."

"And she's with the little guy?"

I shrug. "What can I say, opposites attract, but they're perfect for each other. She once kicked his ass in high school but now they're head over heels in love."

"So, the other one is yours. The football player. Excuse, me, *the tight end*."

"Damn, your mind is in the gutter. But yeah, he's mine. Ryan's my high school sweetheart. I've known him since we were little."

"Well, he's hot. I hope you took him home and ravished him."

As if on cue, Trip stops by, leans down, and kisses Aspen on the cheek. "Hey, babe. Wanna go to lunch?"

"Sure," she says. "I can be free." She shoots me a wink that tells me she's cutting another class.

He looks over at me. "Hi, Jillian. You doing okay?"

"Sure, Trip. You?"

"A lot better since you introduced me to Aspen. I owe you big time."

I cover my mouth as I yawn. "Oh, excuse me. Consider it a random act of kindness."

He studies my face. "You look a little tired, Jillian. Late night, hungover, or both?"

"Neither," I say. "Just a dream that made for a restless night. My dreams are very real. Very lucid." I look right into his eyes. "Sometimes they're a bit frustrating, if you know what I mean.

Like when you wake up and things aren't resolved."

His eyes widen a bit. "I'm, uh, one of those people who never remembers dreams. They're like soap bubbles that pop when I wake up."

I study his face and know he's lying. Time to go fishing for more info. "I guess you're stuck with only daydreams then, huh?"

I bit of color rushes into his face. "Yeah, I guess."

Bus-ted.

He locks eyes with me for a brief moment and I can tell he remembers every detail. And that he's daydreaming about me as well. I keep telling myself it's all the work of the dream weaver, but it feels so right. I gotta get outta here. "Well, I'm gonna be late for class," I say as I get up, even though I don't have a class. "You two have fun."

I walk away, happy that their relationship is going well.

But wondering if I still have a chance with him.

Chapter 13

Fuzzball hands each of us a copy of his research as we all sit around my living room. Everyone is here but Sebastien, though I've already talked to him about recent events. "Unfortunately, we cannot find any birth certificate proving Cruise had a baby," says the detective, sitting on the fireplace hearth. "There are several possible explanations. She could have given birth out of the country. Or with her family's deep pockets, someone could have been paid off to make the records go away. The child could have been given up for adoption. It might not even be alive. However..."

I sit up straight. "However?"

"Cruise did basically go off the grid for several years during her early twenties. Since her family was high profile society and an out of wedlock baby would have been quite the scandal, she might have been sent away or even exiled from the family. Bottom line, she more than likely had a kid but we can't find it. Maybe we never will."

"Appreciate you trying," I say. I quickly scan the sheet to find out when Cruise disappeared, hoping against hope it's after my father left so my mother won't get another dagger in the heart. But the period begins a few years before he took off and ends a few years after. So there's no way of knowing when their affair started. Or how long it lasted. For all I know they were still lovers when we fried his brain. And if so, she would be the woman scorned, but not by a man.

By us.

Fuzzball continues. "Now, as to what the dream weaver did to you by putting you in someone else's dream... Sebastien says there's nothing we can do right now, but they're working on some theories regarding the rapid eye movement that accompanies dreams. They might be able to create some sort of alarm that wakes you up when you start dreaming. I'm sorry, Jillian, I know this is frustrating for you and I wish I had better news."

I exhale deeply. "I guess I'll have to deal with it until we take her down. Hopefully it won't be too long."

Ryan leans over and pats the top of my hand, then entwines his fingers with mine. I gulp and my eyes mist a bit as I'm still overcome with guilt about my feelings for Trip. But I can't let it show. I've told Ryan about being sent into Trip's dream but lied about what happened, that Trip tried to convince me to heal my father. He bought it, along with the theory that Cruise is also controlling Trip's dreams and therefore he is an unwilling participant. It helps a great deal that he saw Aspen all over him at the dance, so Roxanne's suggestion was definitely a good one.

Still, I hate lying to someone I love, especially when it concerns my infatuation with another guy. And my mother is convinced that's all it is. Infatuation. Unfortunately, the images from that dream have been playing on an infinite loop in my head and are having the desired effect. If the dream weaver wants me to obsess about Trip, her plan is working. It's all I can do to focus on the fact that I love Ryan and that my mind and emotions are being manipulated. Throw jealousy into the mix, and my brain is tied in an emotional Gordian knot.

"You know, Jillian," says Jake, "you might not have to deal with it."

"You got a magic potion?" asks Roxanne.

Jake shakes his head and leans forward. "No, listen. What's

been the dream weaver's main objective all along? To break the four of us all up, right? Divide and conquer. She knows when we work together we're powerful enough to take down anyone, and she's afraid. She won't move forward with whatever her plan is until she's made a dent in our team. Which means she's going to continue manipulating Jillian's dreams."

"We already know that. What's your point?" asks Ryan.

"My point is that she's going to keep screwing with Jillian's head until she breaks up your relationship. Or until *she thinks she's done it*."

"Are you suggesting what I think you're suggesting?" asks Mom.

Jake nods. "Yeah." He looks at me and Ryan. "You two have to break up."

"No!" we both say in unison.

"Not really," says Jake. "Hear me out. You have to do something so Cruise *thinks* you're broken up. Once she thinks she's achieved her goal she'll stop with the dream tricks. At least I'd bet that she will."

"How exactly do you propose we do this?" I ask.

"Look, Cruise is coming back to town this week to do a press conference on her identity card project, and she's doing it at our school. You two need to go. At some point when you're nearby you guys get into a fake argument, make a loud scene, something like that. Something that shows you aren't getting along. One of you says you're done and storms off. When she sees that, she'll think you've broken up and she'll back off. Pleasant dreams, Jillian."

They're already too damn pleasant. That's the problem.

Fuzzball scratches his chin. "It could work. I vote we give it a try. If it doesn't work, we haven't lost anything."

Roxanne raises one finger. "There's a possible flaw in the plan. Cruise may have minions around the school. In fact, considering the fact that she's nailed several male students in her office lair I'm sure she does. Suppose someone sees Jillian and Ryan together after they supposedly break up and tell her?"

"Jillian and Ryan can't be seen together in public," says Jake. "At least not till we take Cruise down."

Ryan puts an arm around my shoulder, pulls me close and shakes his head. "No, I'm not staying away from Jillian. We all need to stick together. That's the whole point. This has the same effect as breaking us up for real."

"No, it doesn't, because you don't have to stay away from her," says Jake. "She can be in two places at once, remember? You avoid each other during the day and in public places, then at night she beams over to your place or wherever. As long as it's not a public place."

I begin to slowly nod. This actually could work. I turn to Ryan. "What the hell. I'm game if you are."

"You sure?"

I give him a soulful look which I know he cannot resist. "Sweetie, these dreams are killin' me. I'm afraid to go to sleep at night."

"Okay, Sparks. But if we're gonna do this we'll need to rehearse breaking up."

"That's it!" I try my best to glare at Ryan as we stand in the center of the living room. "I've had it with your jealousy! We're through!"

And everyone cracks up. Ryan doubles over laughing.

"What? What did I do wrong?" I ask.

Roxanne is laughing so hard she has to wipe the tears from her eyes. "You're not exactly selling it."

I put my hands on my hips. "I yelled. You told me to yell and I yelled at him."

"Yeah, but you look like an angry Strawberry Shortcake while you're doing it."

"Well, dammit, I'm sorry. I can't help the way I look. And I've never been mad at Ryan. This is hard for me."

"It's gonna be hard for me not to laugh," says Ryan. I put out my lower lip and he gives me a quick hug, patting me on the back.

"It's okay, Sparks. You're just not cut out to be a bitch. Thank God." He pulls back and looks at me. "I hate to be cliché, but... you're awfully cute when you're angry."

This breaks everyone up, even me.

If nothing else, this "rehearsal" is lightening the mood significantly. For the first time in a while we're having fun.

Roxanne gets up and shoves me aside. "Okay, my dear friend, watch and learn. This is Pissed Off 101. Pay attention, there will be a test later. First, you begin with the death stare." She narrows her dark eyes at Ryan and he backs up a step.

"Whoa," he says. "Remind me to never to get on your bad side."

"Trust me, I learned my lesson a long time ago," says Jake.

Roxanne pulls me by the shoulders so I'm in front of Ryan. "Now you try it."

I shrug as she moves behind Ryan to watch. "Okay." I close my eyes a bit as I stare at him.

"Now you look like a squinting chipmunk," says Rox. "This isn't gonna work. You're just too damn cute with those freckles."

I throw my hands up. "I give up. Maybe he needs to break up with me instead of the other way around. How about that? Then I can play hurt instead of angry."

Mom chimes in. "Sweetie, you're not getting in the right mood to play the role."

"What, you're Steven Spielberg now?"

"Don't think of being mad at Ryan, focus on things that make you angry. What pisses you off the most?"

"I'm not stacked like Roxanne."

Rox actually blushes at that comment.

"Be serious."

"Fine. Cruise pisses me off. My father pisses me off. What they're doing to me and all of us pisses me off."

"She's getting it," says Rox, studying my face. "Okay, Meryl Streep, let's see you sell it."

Mom nods. "Right, focus on your real anger. Look at Ryan, but pretend you're talking to them."

I try and it comes out better. Ryan tries to yell at me but isn't very convincing either as he looks like he'd rather kiss me than walk away.

Finally Rox tells us to stop. "This isn't gonna work with you two. But I have an idea that *will* work."

I have to admit Roxanne's plan is brilliant. And I know she can pull it off.

My only question is what happens if it works.

If Cruise stops manipulating my dreams, will my interest in Trip disappear? Will that "virus" she planted in my head be gone? And will the memories of my sexy dream vanish with it?

Inquiring minds wanna know.

The meeting hall is decorated with red, white and blue bunting and about two hundred students are in attendance for Cruise's visit. Having finished spewing her propaganda about the card while showing off a giant version on an easel, she wraps up her speech to polite applause. She walks away from the podium and is making her way through the crowd, shaking hands with administrators, teachers and students. The four of us have a small table in the back and are waiting until she gets a little closer.

"You ready?" asks Roxanne.

"Ready as I'll ever be," I say, my heart rate kicking up a notch. "But this still feels weird."

"Don't take anything personally," says Ryan. "Remember that nothing I say is true."

"I know. It's still hard even *thinking* you're mad at me."

"I feel the same way, Sparks. But I'll see you tonight, one way or the other."

Roxanne turns to him. "Ryan, you sure you know your lines?"

He nods. "I think we've rehearsed enough."

"Good." She turns to Jake. "Okay, little one, start making your way to Mrs. Robinson and lure her over."

"I'm just a piece of cougar bait to you." Jake looks a little nervous, as being the lure around a woman who's both a siren and a dream weaver is dangerous. Plus, he knows how close he came to being dragged into her lair and being tied up or hung from a trapeze or whatever. "Just make sure you remember to get me outta here before she gets her clutches into me. That cat has big claws."

"Not a problem," says Ryan. "I got your back."

Rox glares at the woman. "Normally I'd say I'd kick her ass."

"Too risky, Rox," says Jake. "My muse needs to stay safe."

She runs her hands through his hair and kisses him. "That's why I love you, little one."

Jake gets up and heads toward the long table that's filled with drinks and hors d'oeuvres. Cruise is still surrounded, busy chatting with supporters as she moves toward the center of the room. Jake stops at the back of the crowd, raises his hand and waves at her. She spots him and makes eye contact.

She perks up immediately and moves in his direction.

And toward us.

"Ready?" asks Rox.

"Get it over with," I say. "Rip the bandage off."

Roxanne and Ryan stand up and move toward each other as Cruise is about to reach Jake. "Look, you don't own her!" says Rox, raising her voice and jamming her finger in his chest as she invokes the Sicilian death stare and cranks up the Brooklyn accent. A few people look in our direction. "She is *not* your personal possession."

"Yeah, well I'm sick of her talking about other guys," says Ryan, glaring at Roxanne. "She's *my* girlfriend."

"What, you think 'cause you're her boyfriend you can put her in a box? I got your box *right here*. She's allowed to have male friends, you know. Or do you expect her to go through life only talking to women with blinders on?"

"What about love, honor and obey?"

Their voices are carrying and the murmur of the crowd dies down as this is now a full-fledged scene. Everyone is now looking at them. Cruise and Jake are a few feet apart, but both have stopped to watch the show.

"*Obey? Obey?* First of all, youse two aren't married." She waves her finger back and forth like a pissed off teacher. "No, no, no." She moves closer so that they're nose to nose. "Second, this aint nineteen fifty and she's not gonna rush to get your slippers when you get home. And if you two *were* to get married, which looks to be as much of a long shot as the Jets winnin' the Super Bowl, who the hell declared *you* lord and mastuh?"

(Speaking of master, Rox is a master at this. Or in her case, mastuh.)

He turns to me, hands on hips. "So, I suppose you agree with her?"

I try my best to look indignant as I stand and fold my arms because I'm shaking, ready to deliver my one line. My heart slams against my chest even though I know this isn't real. I stick my chin out. "Yeah. If I wanna have male friends, I have the right. And right now I want to keep my male friends."

Ryan glares at me and waves me away. "Fine, go spend time with some other guys. In fact, you'll have plenty of time because we're done!" He turns and storms off as Roxanne moves over to me and wraps an arm around my shoulders. I bury my head in her chest and pretend to cry as she strokes my hair. I'm actually shaking.

"You're better off, honey," she says, then turns to the crowd that is staring at us. "Hey, why doncha take a picture? It'll last longer!" They turn away and back to the special guest.

Roxanne escorts me out of the room. I look to the side and see two things.

Ryan grabbing Jake by the arm and pulling him outta there.

And Cruise smiling.

"Be there in two minutes. Wanted to give you a heads up." I hit the send button and the text is on its way.

Ryan replies almost immediately. "Make it one minute. Two is too long to wait."

I'm unable to contain a huge smile as I stretch out on my bed, close my eyes and focus on his dorm room.

And when I appear, for once I don't scare the hell out of him. I leap into his arms and hug him tight.

"Wow, I missed you too," he says. "What's it been, four hours?"

I kiss him and wrap my legs around his waist. "I'm so sorry, Ryan."

"About what?" He loops his arms underneath my hips to hold me up.

"You know. Our breakup."

"Uh, you *do* know that wasn't real. I would never break up with you."

"I know, but it felt real. It made me feel bad anyway. I don't ever want to be mad at you. Damn, I'd be a horrible lawyer if I'm that bad at confrontation. I was shaking really bad."

"Yeah, it felt strange to me too. But if this is the reaction I get, maybe we should break up more often."

"Smart ass."

"So, do you feel any different?"

"You're the one holding me, you tell me."

"I dunno... you might have gained a few pounds."

"Hey!"

"Kidding." He taps my head. "I meant do you feel any different up here?"

"Not really, but too early to tell. I'll let you know what I wake up."

"I'm sure you'll have pleasant dreams. By the way, I found it very interesting that you're taking the *obey* thing out of the wedding vows."

I lean back a bit. "Oh, so you think the woman should obey?"

"I was planning on obeying *you*. Will you be wanting your slippers as soon as you get home, or after dinner?"

He makes me smile like no one else. "Damn, I love you."

He shrugs. "Yeah, I know." He nods at his desk and a pizza box with steam coming out of it. "I got dinner. C'mon, it'll get cold."

"You have a girl wrapped around you like a snake and you wanna stop for dinner?"

"It's pizza. I'm a guy in college, pizza is my life."

"So, you'd rather eat pizza than make out with me?"

"The pizza will get cold. You obviously won't."

"Does this have anything to do with the fact that I can't eat as a projection?"

"Yeah. More for me."

"Well, okay. I wouldn't want you to starve." I drop out of his arms and sit on the side of the bed as he moves toward the pizza. "So, I talked to Rox, and so far Jake has no symptoms from being close to Cruise."

"Good, I'm glad we got him outta there in time." He grabs a slice from the box and takes a bite. "Listen, Sparks," he says through the pizza, "I got close enough to her for a few seconds to pick up some stuff."

"Really. Do tell."

"She was happy to see our argument. She totally bought it."

"Yeah, I got that from the look on her face."

"And she feels she can now move forward."

"With what?"

He shakes his head. “Don’t know. That’s all I got because we were rushing to get out of there. But the bottom line is that she feels invincible now.”

Chapter 14

Three weeks later I'm sleeping like a baby. No more bad dreams, no more dreams suitable for late night cable (that is now Mom's department), no more finding myself in someone else's dream, no more thinking I'm dreaming when I'm actually awake. Haven't even needed to check Carrielle's ring. So our fake breakup worked.

Meanwhile, Trip Logan now looks at me like he barely knows me and has become totally entranced with Aspen. Which is good news, of course. Obviously the dream weaver also stopped manipulating him when she realized he was no longer necessary. Whatever he might have felt for me, real or imagined, is out of his system.

As for getting Trip Logan out of *my* system, well, that's another story. If you're familiar with the term "carrying a torch," well, I'm hauling around an Olympic one. Much as I try to avoid him, the campus is small, and every time I see the guy my heart skips a beat.

The Summit confirms that the so-called "virus" put in my head by the dream weaver is gone as it isn't showing up in my brain waves. Everything is back to normal in that department. Unfortunately the memories resulting from said virus live on. And on. And on. Not a day goes by that I don't relive what happened in Trip's dream, even if it's for a few seconds. Or I daydream about him carrying me to the infirmary. Or making out with him at the dance. And there's still the longing I feel whenever I see him and

Aspen together. She's such a sweet girl and yet when she talks about Trip I get jealous, even though I have a wonderful guy of my own. Thankfully, she's still hot for him, their relationship is a serious one and he doesn't seem the least bit interested in me even when I've made serious eye contact. (Just to check, of course. A girl has to keep on top of things. Of course I know it's the jealousy talking, and it's not really me.) Still, I wish the residual effects of the virus would disappear. Everyone at The Summit assures me they will.

I'll believe it when I see it.

Of course, I haven't told Ryan about the dream and never will. He's been through enough and has been an absolute saint through all this. The last thing he needs is a recap of how I ravished Trip in a dream and how the guy does things to me physically that he doesn't. Meanwhile, my relationship with him is strong, especially considering the fact that I'm beaming my alter ego over to his dorm room on a nightly basis. Sure, I miss going out to dinner with him, and when we want to see a movie I go with Roxanne and he goes with Jake, then we all meet up when the lights go down in the theater. And he wants the real Jillian in his bed, not the facsimile. Though the facsimile does enjoy her little sleepovers even though the minute I actually fall asleep I zip back to my real body. Just once I'd like to wake up in his arms instead of hugging a pillow. I keep telling myself it won't be forever, but I want to get back to a normal life.

And considering what happened this morning, it shouldn't be too long. One way or another.

Cruise's bill on the identity card sailed through Congress and was signed into law. I did a little research and found that every male member of the House and Senate voted for it, the only dissent coming from women. They oughta call her the singing Senator considering she got support from guys in the other party who should be her mortal enemy. Every time she makes a speech she hums a little as she steps to the microphone, and the men in the press corps become deer in the headlights lobbing softball questions. She's getting the project fast tracked in the hopes of getting the cards into the hands of the citizens in a matter of weeks.

Which means we'll be locking horns soon. So there's light at the end of the tunnel.

Then again, sometimes the light is a speeding train.

Thanks to his Men in Black friends in the federal government, Fuzzball has managed to score some of the prototype equipment that will put the identity card system into place and has hauled it over to The Summit so their band of merry geeks can figure out what it's going to do to people. Though I already have a pretty good idea. I'm betting that it's similar to what the cell phone did, but if it's part of that "phase two" of my father's original plan known as Babylon, it could be something worse. Mom keeps reminding me that not everyone had one of his cell phones, while every man, woman and child in the country will be issued an identity card.

And have to register in person using a fingerprint.

Sebastien is convinced that's the key as we all sit patiently while the geek squad works on the project. The cards are the size of a credit card, with a magnetic strip across the back and a space for a photo, signature and fingerprint on the front. To get the thing "registered" the card slides into a machine while you place your thumb on what looks like a track pad of a laptop. It's all hooked up to a computer much larger than the average desktop.

Probably because it's more than an average computer since, you know, the average computer doesn't access your brain waves and turn you into a pod person. According to Fuzzball's contacts, it's the most powerful digital device owned by the government. Once again, your tax dollars at work.

One of the middle-aged tech guys in a white lab coat who has been hovering over the system turns to Sebastien. "We should have results in a few moments."

Sebastien stops pacing and nods. "Very well."

"So, is this something we can crash like the cell phone?" I ask.

"Upload a virus and be done with it?"

"Don't know," says Fuzzball. "But I would guess not since we've been down that road before and they're probably ready for it. I'll take the results back to my guy at Homeland Security and see what the deal is. They still have the virus we used last time, but the bad guys have surely learned from previous experience and might have adapted the system to make it virus proof and completely secure. We all know how fast technology can change and designers can adapt. And remember, Cruise is a member of the Senate now, so she has access to the same high tech government stuff I do. Probably more, since she's the brains behind this gizmo."

The computer beeps and a printer that is hooked up to the computer starts spitting out several sheets of paper. The techie grabs them, takes a look and hands it to Sebastien. "It's definitely here," says the techie, exhaling audibly as he runs his hand over his bald head. He points to a spot on the paper with a pencil. "Right there. As you suspected."

"What's there?" I ask.

"Your father's memory engrams," says Sebastien, nodding as he studies the paper.

"His *what*?" asks Ryan.

"They're called *engrams*," says the tech guy. "Many think the concept is hypothetical, but it's not. In simple terms, some of your father's memories are stored in the master computer. Check that... not necessarily his memories, like things he did as a child, or specific experiences, but his basic beliefs. Right from wrong, love versus hate, that sort of thing. The basic concepts that form his personality. Instead of basic mathematical formulas the computer's decision making process is based on ethical beliefs."

"Wonderful," says Roxanne. "Just what we need. The whole country getting a new definition of right and wrong from your father. I'm guessing he comes down on the side of wrong."

"So that's why someone copied his brain," says Jake. "To basically put his agenda into everyone's head. This is Project Babylon."

"Yes, it appears so," says Sebastien, handing the printout back to the tech guy.

"I wonder how it would have tied in with the cell phone project?" asks Ryan.

"We may never know," says the techie. "My theory is that the cell phone was part of a mind control experiment, to see if it actually worked. This takes it to another level by using engrams, which are already present in the card before it is activated. Think of it as a basic operating system that's already installed in a computer when you buy it. Everything works in conjunction with the operating system. In this case, that system is an actual copy of a brain."

Sebastien nods as he gives me a serious look. "We had a feeling they were going to incorporate it into their next project when his brain was copied. Embedding your father's basic beliefs into every citizen will have a devastating effect."

"But there are little things as well," says the techie. "Things that are deeply embedded in the mind that may surface, things they don't intend to see. Memories that are physical, not mental."

"Not sure I understand," says Roxanne.

"For instance, if you burned your hand as a child, that hand might always flinch when someone touched it, even though it's now perfectly fine. You might not even notice that you do it. It's a muscle memory thing, and even though your hand doesn't have brain cells, it sort of remembers that it was hurt. That type of response can be carried in memory engrams in a very powerful way. How strong these engrams will be is anyone's guess, and I would surmise that it would affect different people in different ways."

"Are you saying," says Ryan, "that some of the physical traits of Jillian's father could be transferred as well?"

"It's very possible. In fact, I would bet on it. Of course, we'd have to know what those traits were to recognize them."

I turn to my mother. "Mom?"

Mom looks to the ceiling, trying to remember. "Let's see. He had a bit of a twitch in his left eye. Other than that, I can't think of anything other than he liked to snap his fingers a lot."

I'm beginning to understand this as I turn back to the tech guy. "So, basically when people get their identity card, some of my father's core beliefs will be transferred to them?"

He nods. "Yes. The pad on which the thumb is placed is not only a scanner, but a connective device that goes directly to the brain using the network of nerves in our bodies. People will think they are simply being fingerprinted. In reality, they are being programmed with a new set of beliefs. But until we actually test this on a human, we won't know what the effect will be. Though I'm guessing the others have already tested it and it works. And then there's the other problem."

"What's that?" asks Fuzzball.

"If the process can be reversed. What's embedded could be permanent."

The ride home is taking forever. We've been stuck in traffic and for some reason the people who run the state's toll booths think they only need to staff two people on weekends while shutting down most of the automated EZ Pass lanes. Cars are making the slow crawl as people wait in line to pay ridiculous amounts of money for the privilege of driving in the northeast.

"What is this, a Wal-Mart express line?" asks Mom, who's driving. Fuzzball is in the passenger seat doing something on his laptop while Roxanne, Jake and I fill the back seat of our family land yacht. Of course since I'm the shortest and smallest, I'm stuck in the middle. The curse of the vertically challenged. Though if Ryan hadn't stayed behind to work on something with Sebastien, I'd be on his lap and not complaining.

Jake exhales and looks at his watch. "We've now been here twenty minutes just to pay the toll. Is it just me, or is there something very wrong with a society in which you have to wait in line to give the government money?"

"This is ridiculous," says Rox. "Would it kill them to open the

EZ Pass lanes? They don't need humans to run those."

I look at the line of red lights over eight closed lanes. "Hey, Jake, you think you can hit the booths from here?"

"It's a long way away. Why?"

"I was thinking you could change all the lights to green and turn on the booths. Then everyone in front of us would move and we could get the hell out of here."

"Great idea," says Rox. She reaches over and pats Jake on the knee. "Give it a shot, little one, we got nothing to lose."

"Okay," says Jake. The telekinetic raises his hand and points a finger at the line of toll booths. One of the lights flickers briefly from red to green but ends up back on red. He tries again, but the end result is the same. "I could do it if we were closer. I don't have enough juice from this far out."

Mom manages to creep forward a few feet. "C'mon, try it again," I say. "One more time."

Jake goes through the process again with similar results, though the light stays green a bit longer. His face tightens as he focuses on the task.

I rest my hand lightly on his shoulder. "C'mon, Jake, you can do it. You're almost there."

And suddenly his eyes widen and all the lights turn green.

The parking lot turns into a road rally as cars race to the open lanes. Mom turns into a NASCAR driver and screeches her way forward, cutting people off and getting a few extended middle fingers from other drivers in the process.

I pat him on the back. "Jake, you rock."

"You did it!" says Rox.

Jake turns and looks at Roxanne wide-eyed. "No, I didn't."

"Sure you did," says Mom, as she navigates her way toward the booth. "All the lanes turned on."

Jake shakes his head. "Not what I meant." He turns to me. "*I* didn't do it. *We* did."

"What are you talking about?" I ask.

"I couldn't do it alone, Jillian. Until you put your hand on my shoulder. All of a sudden I got this rush of energy, like my power was multiplied ten times. I could feel it coming from you. I *know* it was you."

Fuzzball closes his laptop and turns around. "Jillian, what were you thinking when you touched Jake?"

I shrug. "I was hoping he could get the lights changed so we could get the hell out of this traffic jam."

He nods slowly as he looks at Jake. "And you actually felt her power coming into you?"

"Absolutely. Like it ran right into my mind. All of a sudden I could focus like never before. I've never felt so powerful. The rest of the world disappeared and all I could see were the tollbooths."

"You know what this means," says Mom, as she makes her way through the booth.

"What?" I ask.

"It's obvious," says Roxanne. "You not only have the power to heal, but to increase the power of whoever you touch."

Chapter 15

I look at my ticket stub as I walk through the concourse and figure I need to find my seat. The weather is perfect: not a cloud in the sky, temperatures in the seventies, a light offshore breeze. A vendor passes me and the smell of hot dogs fills my lungs. But this is old Shea Stadium, famous for cold frankfurters on stale buns and food that would give any lunch lady a run for her money, so I resist the temptation. I find my section, right behind third base, and head down the steps to my row, which is right on the rail near the dugout. The sellout crowd applauds as the Mets take the field.

I turn into the row and find Carrielle already seated. "I was hoping you'd be here. You always pick such nice places to meet."

"I want our meetings to be as relaxing as possible. I know of your fondness for baseball."

"Yeah, nice to go to a game in the middle of November." Carrielle hands me a soda and a bag of peanuts. "And you know what I like."

"Your obsession with food amuses me, Jillian."

"Yeah, but it's a really good obsession." I rip open the bag. "Salted in the shell. My favorite. Thank you."

He nods. "You're very welcome."

I crack open a peanut shell and pop the nut in my mouth, savoring the salty treat. It's actually fresh, a far cry from the stuff they used to sell here for outrageous prices. "So, when were you gonna tell me I had yet another power? That might have come in handy last spring."

"You did not have that power then, Jillian. You must understand that you are still evolving, still developing your powers."

"So my ability to amplify the powers of others is something brand new?"

He touches my forehead with two fingers, which gives me peace. And also tells me something troubling is heading my way. "We are given gifts as we need them. You did not need this gift before."

His answer would normally make my blood pressure spike but I never feel any stress during my times with the angel, especially after he's done the peace number on my head. "Which means I'm going to need this new power."

He nods. "You are facing a great enemy, Jillian. Not necessarily more powerful than your father, but perhaps more dangerous. She is ruthless, without conscience, and will let nothing stand in her way. As she has already demonstrated."

"What can you tell me about her?"

"As before, dark forces prevent us from reading her. And those who follow her. But what she is doing can be very damaging to the fabric of society, which is very fragile to begin with."

I turn and look out at the game. The Mets make a couple of incredible defensive plays, something that rarely happens in real life. "Nice fantasy, Carrielle."

He shrugs and smiles. "Wouldn't want your favorite team to lose."

"How come you can't fix this team in real life? I mean, geez, throw us a couple of decent outfielders. Let them make the playoffs once in a while."

"Sports are not a priority in my kingdom. They are simply for your entertainment."

"Yeah, well, the Mets are entertaining all right, but not in a good way." I take a sip of the ice cold soda to wash down the salty nuts. "Carrielle, I need to ask you about sirens."

"Yes. They are very powerful and can render men mad. Song is usually a gift, but they do not use it in the manner it was intended."

"I'm really worried about Roxanne. I was told that Cruise actually killed a muse once."

"A terrible sin," he says, his eyes suddenly moist. "A muse is such a special creature, one who bestows gifts of inspiration and beauty. To take the life of one..."

His voice trails off and he looks down at the ground. I rest my hand on his shoulder. "Can you tell me how she killed the muse so it doesn't happen to Roxanne? All I know is that the siren pretended to want a session with the muse."

"Yes. The siren tricked her, told her she wanted to be inspired. When the muse entered her mind the siren sang subconsciously, paralyzing her. She was not expecting to be in a battle, for as you know, a muse can defeat a siren."

"So the legend is true."

"Yes. But in this case, the siren was extremely powerful. And with the battle being waged in the subconscious, the muse was not able to defeat her. Alas, she is here with the angels."

"That doesn't make me feel any better about Roxanne. So what do we do, Carrielle?"

"The key word is *we*, Jillian. You have a new gift. I suggest you use it."

The envelope from the federal government makes my blood pressure spike. Because I know what's inside.

The ID cards from hell.

Everyone is receiving them this week, with instructions to take them to an "activation center" so that you can be registered. And presumably, be turned into one of millions of minions of my father complete with his dark personality traits.

The sonofabitch is basically out of commission, and still he's causing trouble.

Sebastien has instructed us not to even touch the things,

especially the part of the card where your thumbprint will go. The techies at The Summit seem to think that even without the activation process the card could possibly transmit my father's memory engrams to anyone who touches one. So the people who don't bother to get activated might be controlled to some degree anyway.

But trust me, people will be lining up to get the thing turned on. Cruise has gotten corporate sponsors to offer freebies to everyone who gets the card activated. So you can sell your soul for complimentary cell phone minutes or a bunch of free music downloads, the latter giveaway designed to appeal to my generation. Sell your soul, get the new single by your favorite artist. Such a deal!

And as I turn on the local news, I see it's actually working.

A live shot from a helicopter shows a long line stretching for blocks in midtown Manhattan.

A shot from the street reveals that most of the people are young.

Mom brings her coffee in from the kitchen and sits down next to me. "Uh-oh. Big turnout, huh?"

"Unfortunately. The power of free stuff trumps all."

The shot cuts to a blonde female reporter who has a reputation as an airhead. She's inside the activation center with a flurry of activity going on behind her. "You think the card will make her less stupid?"

"Nah, just stupid and mean."

The reporter nods as she takes a question from the anchor. "Yes, there's quite a turnout on day one of the ID card activation, as you saw from our shots outside." She walks over to a large leather chair that is currently occupied by a grungy twenty-something who looks as though bathing is not on his to-do list. "Here's how it works. You take a seat and put one thumb on the card, and the other on this scanning pad, which is connected to the master registry computer. Then a technician activates the card and you're in the system. It's very simple and painless."

"Yeah, you're in the system, all right," says Mom.

"The whole thing takes about a minute," says the reporter. She turns to the guy in the chair. "So what brought you out this morning?"

He nods at his iPod. "Free tunes."

"Do you feel anything?"

He shakes his head. "Nah, it's no different than when I got fingerprinted after my last arrest. I figured they already had me on file, so what the hell. They already know where to find me."

The computer beeps. The technician pulls the card from the machine and hands it to the guy. "You're all set," he says.

Mom fires the remote at the television and turns down the sound. "And now we wait."

"How long do you think it'll take to have an effect?"

She shrugs. "No way of knowing. But it will be obvious when we see it."

The guy gets out of the chair, smiles for the camera and puts his headphones back on.

His left eye twitches and he starts to snap his fingers.

"And there it is," says Mom.

With Project Babylon underway I figure there's no time to waste in taking Carrielle's advice. I need to find out how to amplify the powers of my friends and how much I can affect them.

Ryan sneaked through the back yard to get into my house and has joined Jake in our living room seated facing the front window. I'm meeting Roxanne later to work with her powers since that will be crucial to taking on Cruise, but for now we're going to test the guys.

"Who wants to go first?" I ask.

Jake raises his hand. "I've been waiting all day for this. Let's rock."

"Okay." I crouch down and look through our living room window down the street. A full city block away I see the familiar pair of sneakers hanging over a power line. The damn things have been there for a year, and annoy the hell out of me since this is such a nice neighborhood. "See the sneakers?" I ask, pointing at them.

"Yeah. No way can I get those. Too far away."

"Alas, your human set of jumper cables is right here." I take his hand and focus on sending energy into his body. "Get the damn things off the power line."

Jake points at them with his free hand and narrows his eyes. His face tightens.

The sneakers begin to sway back and forth.

"Need a little more juice," says Jake.

I focus harder and the sneakers suddenly fly off the line and land on the ground. I jump up and down and clap. "You did it!"

"*We* did it," says Jake. "Damn, I can't believe I could hit something that far away."

"Try something farther," says Ryan. "And harder."

Jake looks out the window and points. "Old man Ferguson's Mercedes in the driveway."

I see the gleaming red sedan a block and a half away. "What, you gonna drive it?"

"Nah, just set off the alarm. The old guy always yells at you if you even get within breathing distance of that car. He's like Clint Eastwood telling kids to get off his lawn. Let's freak him out. I'll need enough to give the car a good shove."

"This is beginning to sound like the old Jake," says Ryan.

"What can I say, I still love a good practical joke," he says, with that familiar sinister smile we knew before Roxanne tamed him. Though it did make a brief return in my Modern Lit class. "If this Mercedes is rockin' don't come knockin'."

I go through the routine, giving him my power. He points, focuses, and the car begins to sway like two teenagers are in the back seat. An ear-piercing alarm goes off, bringing the owner out in a flash. He frantically looks for the culprit who isn't there. We share a good laugh as the guy waves a baseball bat in the air, yells "Damn kids!", gives up and goes back inside.

"That was hilarious!" I say.

"How are you feeling?" asks Ryan.

"Fine," I say. "But that wasn't anything critical."

"Let's get him again," says Jake.

"Later," I say. "Ryan's turn." I see a couple walking down the street, moving away from us, perhaps half a block away, and point at them. "Read their minds."

"I think they are seriously out of my range, Sparks."

"Maybe not." I stand behind him, put my hands on his shoulders and send energy into his body. Ryan closes his eyes. I keep sending him energy for a minute, then he opens his eyes which are filled with wonder.

"Wow."

"You got something?" asks Jake.

"I got everything! I've never gone that far into someone's head before. And I got *both* of them."

Roxanne welcomes the client, a short, pudgy middle-aged screenwriter named Douglas. He has thick salt-and-pepper hair and a neatly trimmed beard to match.

But the best way to describe his look is desperate.

His deep-set dark eyes are filled with defeat, his shoulders slumped. He reminds me of the commuting undead you see at Grand Central waiting for the train home.

Roxanne leads him to the couch where I'm waiting. "Douglas, this is Jillian, my best friend."

"Hello," he says, without much emotion, as he extends his hand.

"Hi, Douglas." His handshake is weak, without life.

"Jillian will be taking notes on our session today," says Rox, handing me a clipboard for effect.

"Sure," says Douglas, who sits on the couch.

Roxanne sits opposite him. "So what can I do for you today?"

"Well, as I told you on the phone, I'm a screenwriter and I haven't had a sale for almost ten years, since *Moonwalk*."

My eyes widen. "You wrote *Moonwalk*? I love that movie! And that plot twist at the end... I never saw it coming!"

He forces a smile. "Thank you, you're very kind. Anyway, I haven't been able to come up with a decent plot since. And if I don't write something marketable soon, I fear my agent will drop me. And without an agent, I have no access to getting my work to Hollywood, so my career would effectively be over."

Roxanne nods and pats his hand. "I understand. You need a kick-ass plot."

"Yes," he says. "Something that will get me back on the A-list again. Sydney Jensen told me you did wonders for her career. That you inspired her to write *Breakthrough Day*."

"That's nice to hear. I like working with Syd. But the talent part is all hers. All I do is inspire."

"That's what I need. Divine inspiration or any other kind."

Roxanne explains the process and tells the client that sometimes the inspiration takes a few days. He asks a few simple questions, then lies back and focuses on her. I'm sitting on a chair next to her with the clipboard in my lap, though I won't be taking notes as it's just for show. She gives me a quick nod and I take her hand. She locks onto the guy as she did with me and after a few moments I can tell she's in his mind.

I focus, sending energy into her body. I have no idea how long this will take.

Five minutes later, she's still locked in and I'm feeling slightly drained. But I've still got plenty of juice, so I send a strong dose into her. Her reaction is noticeable. She sits up straight, eyes getting wider, but still locked with her client.

Thirty seconds later she exhales, blinks several times and turns to me. "Damn, Jillian, what a rush!"

"It worked?"

"Oh, big time." She turns to the client and taps his hand. "Douglas? Douglas?"

His eyes open wide and he smiles at her. "That was incredible!

You gave me the entire plot! Every character, every plot twist, every funny line. You gave me a blockbuster!"

"Seriously?" I ask.

"Everything is clear as a bell. I need to get home and write this down immediately. Roxanne, I can't thank you enough." He takes her hands, his eyes welling up. "You just saved my career. I'm sure of it."

"You saved your own career, Douglas. The story was already in your head. I just helped to get it out."

"Whatever," he says. "Make sure you watch the Academy Awards in a couple of years. I'll be thanking you personally. Right now I gotta call my agent and start writing."

The client is upbeat, a changed man as he shakes my hand and gives Rox a strong hug before leaving. As soon as he shuts the door she turns to me. "Jillian, that was amazing! The most incredible session I've ever had."

"So what happened?"

"Usually when I go into a writer's head there are all sorts of ideas bouncing around, like a bunch of ping pong balls in a lottery drawing. I try to put them in some sort of order and move the best ones to the front of the line. But this guy, oh, *madonne*, what a nightmare in his head. I've never seen such a convoluted mess of ideas, tangents going all over the place."

"So what did you do?"

"Usually with someone this screwed up it takes several sessions to simply weed out all the crap. But it was like I was working at warp speed, deleting the bad stuff and organizing the great ideas which had been buried by his depression. Jillian, he had the plot in his head and I put the whole thing together. I can even tell you what the movie will look like. It's absolutely brilliant."

"That's never happened before?"

“Are you kidding? Honey, you just raised my talent to the tenth power. When I was in his mind, I was in charge. Nothing could have stopped me. And now nothing will.”

Chapter 16

Fuzzball attaches the device that looks like a button to Jake's shirt. "Wow," says Jake. "I'm wired just like on television."

"Don't lose it," says Fuzzball. "These things cost a small fortune." He hands Jake another tiny device. "This goes in your ear." Jake inserts the thing as the detective crosses the hotel room and puts on a headset.

"What's the range on this?" asks Ryan, who is already equipped with the same stuff.

"About a quarter mile," says Fuzzball. "Plenty for our purposes." He adjusts the microphone on the headset. "Can you guys hear me?"

"Loud and clear," says Jake.

"Perfect," says Ryan.

"Okay, talk to me, and just whisper. Jake, you first."

They finish testing the system and we're good to go.

Fuzzball turns to Roxanne. "There's still time if you wanna change your mind."

She shakes her head. "We're doing this. I'm the only one who can stop her."

"She can also kill you," I say, grabbing her forearm.

"Not with my human jumper cables next to me," she says, wrapping one arm around my shoulders.

I turn to Jake. "You okay with all this? You've been awfully quiet."

"You can't exactly stop Roxanne when she's made up her mind. And she does have a bit of a hero complex."

"It's a *heroine* complex," says Rox. "And I'm damn proud of it."

"Yeah," says Jake, "but you're not the one playing the role of cougar bait for Mrs. Robinson. Again."

"Okay, we're good to go," says Fuzzball, setting his audio receiving equipment on a credenza next to three monitors. "And everyone remember, I'll be in the next room if anything goes south. So don't hesitate to call for help."

"Cruise will be the one needing help," says Roxanne.

Jake looks very dapper in his suit and tie as one of the two cameras Fuzzball picks up his arrival in the hotel ballroom. The reception for Senator Cruise is well attended, mostly with high rollers. The room is a sea of expensive suits and cocktail dresses. Bar waiters snake through the crowd carrying trays filled with champagne glasses. The Senator is working the rope line, shaking hands and smiling as she heads toward the podium.

"Mike check, Ryan," says Fuzzball.

"Testing one, two," says Ryan.

"You're good. Jake?"

"Cougar bait to red leader."

"Very funny. You're loud and clear. Be careful, you two. I don't want anyone going rogue."

"I think that's Roxanne's department," says Jake.

"Very funny," says Rox.

Roxanne and I are looking over Fuzzball's shoulders as he watches the two monitors providing a feed from the ballroom. The third screen features a static shot of Cruise's suite next door, which is currently unoccupied. "Here she comes, Jake," says the detective. "Headed right for you. About twenty feet away."

Jake gets up on his toes and looks over the crowd. "I see her," he whispers. "Heading her way."

Cruise has about a dozen hands to shake before she gets to Jake. I reach out, take Roxanne's hand and give it a squeeze. "You got yourself a brave young man out there."

"Yeah. Pretty proud of the little guy. He'd take a bullet for me."

"Join the club."

"Okay," says Fuzzball, "here we go."

The monitor shows Cruise's face lighting up as she spots Jake on the receiving line. She moves through the crowd, takes his hand, shakes it, and places her other hand on top, holding him in place. "Jake, how nice of you to come." Her voice is clear as a bell, picked up by his microphone. Jake, as instructed, gives her the deer in the headlights look.

"I didn't get a chance to talk to you the last time," he says. "I was hoping we might get together later on. Y'know, so we could... talk."

"Yes," she says. Cruise then leans forward and whispers in his ear. "Presidential Suite. Ten o'clock." She leans back and locks eyes with him. "Nice to see you again, Jake." He nods, she smiles and moves on.

"You heard her, right?" asks Jake.

"Copy that," says Fuzzball. "Ryan, whaddaya got?"

The other monitor shows Ryan, wearing thick horn rimmed glasses and dressed as a waiter, following a few feet behind Cruise. "She's going to seduce him."

"Just as we suspected," says Fuzzball.

"One more thing," says Ryan.

"What's that?"

"Now don't freak out when I tell you this. Once she's done with Jake, she plans to take out Roxanne."

We've all been quietly watching Cruise since she arrived in her suite at ten minutes till ten. She disappears into the bathroom for a moment carrying a hanging bag.

"Guess she's slipping into something more comfortable," says Jake.

"That conservative gray suit not turn you on?" asks Roxanne.

"Only if you were the one wearing it."

"Damn, you're good," says Ryan.

"I'm betting a cheap miniskirt and stilettos," I say.

"Nah," says Rox. "Bikini under a sheer negligee."

Fuzzball rolls his eyes. "If you're done with the fashion competition, we need to focus."

"We're just trying to lighten the mood," I say.

"We can pop the champagne later," says the detective. "Or in your case, the Dr. Pepper." He points to the monitor. "Hey, here she comes."

Cruise emerges from the bathroom in a short black leather skirt, matching thigh high boots and a tight gathered red top.

"Skank," says Roxanne.

I add "slut" for good measure.

"Guess she forgot to pack the whip," says Jake.

Fuzzball looks at his watch. "Okay, it's ten o'clock." He turns to Jake. "Off you go to see Mistress Rebecca. She doesn't look like the kind of woman who likes to be kept waiting."

Jake turns and gives Roxanne a hug. "Be careful in there," he says.

"Judging from her outfit, you're the one who needs to be careful."

"Again, only if you were wearing it."

We're all gathered around the monitor as we watch Cruise move toward the door to answer Jake's knock. Roxanne is riveted with her steel glare and a clenched jaw. Both hands are curled into fists. I gently take her forearm. "Stay calm, girl."

"Sicilians don't have that chromosome," she says.

Cruise answers the door and finds a smiling Jake whose jaw drops as he takes in her outfit. She pulls him into the room and hugs him.

Ryan makes a sound like a hungry cat. "Rrrrrowwwwww."

"She sure doesn't waste any time," says Fuzzball, reaching into his bag for some earplugs. He hands one pair to Ryan and keeps one in his hand. "Remember, if we have to go in there, these go in first."

"Gotcha," says Ryan.

Meanwhile, I'm dressed as a room service waitress, black wig, thick glasses, in a uniform borrowed from a hotel. There's also a bottle of champagne chilling in an ice bucket, sitting atop a small rolling cart along with a tray of chocolate dipped strawberries, the sight of which is making me lick my lips. (Hopefully we'll take down Cruise before she has a chance to eat those.) Fuzzball cranks up the audio on the monitor.

"I'm sorry we didn't get to chat last time," says Cruise, running one long red fingernail inside his lapel. "You were such a good student and I've missed talking with you."

"Same here," says Jake. "The teacher who replaced you isn't half as interesting. Or attractive."

Roxanne grimaces at that. "Hey, it's in the script," I say.

"I know. Still pisses me off to hear it."

"Aren't you sweet," says Cruise. "And may I say you clean up pretty well yourself. You look terrific in a suit, young man."

"Thank you, Ms. Cruise."

"Oh, I think we've reached the point where you can call me Rebecca." Cruise takes Jake by the hand and leads him over to the love seat. She sits down and pats the cushion next to her. "So, activated your ID card yet?"

Jake shakes his head. "Mine apparently got lost in the mail. I called the eight hundred number and they told me they would send a replacement immediately. So hopefully I'll get in the system in a couple of days."

"Ah, good."

"So, how's that program going?"

"Very good so far. Firing on all cylinders." She reaches over and runs one hand lightly through his hair. "Though I could use an attractive young person to help with publicity. You know, to reach people your age. I could set it up with the school so you could get college credit. Spend the semester with me in Washington. You'd be the face of the program for your generation."

Jake's eyes widen along with his smile. "Wow, seriously? That would be terrific. What would I have to do?"

"I'll set the wheels in motion tomorrow. You could be in DC by next week." She slides a little closer on the couch. "Can I get you something to drink?"

"Oh, I ordered something sent up," says Jake. "I didn't want to show up empty handed." He checks his watch. "It should be here any minute."

"Well, aren't you a thoughtful young man."

"That's your cue," says Fuzzball. "Go."

"Good luck," says Ryan, giving me a kiss before hugging Roxanne. "We're seconds away if you need us."

"Trust me, we won't," says Roxanne.

I knock softly and say, "Room service," doing my best to disguise my voice.

My heart is pounding as I hear footsteps move toward the door. Roxanne has her back pressed against the hallway wall so Cruise can't see her.

The door opens and I'm face to face with Cruise. She doesn't even bother to study my face, obviously considering me one of the hotel servants. Instead she looks at the ice bucket and the berries. "Ah, champagne. And some other goodies. Do come in."

"Thank you," I say, as I wheel the cart into the room. Jake makes eye contact as I move over toward the couch, with Cruise following me.

"Jake, the strawberries are a nice touch. Thank you."

"I read somewhere they were your favorite."

"You read correctly. I'm an incurable chocoholic."

I park the tray next to the couch, then take a receipt out of my pocket along with a pen and hand it to her. "Please sign."

It's Roxanne's cue to enter the room.

Cruise takes the ticket and the pen which I already know doesn't work since she needs to be distracted for a brief moment. I slide behind her as Roxanne tiptoes into the room. Cruise tries to sign the bill but the pen doesn't write, so she shakes it and scribbles it on the bill, trying to get the ink flowing. By now Roxanne is next to me and I take her hand.

I send all the power I've got into her as Cruise turns to me. "This pen won't—"

Her jaw drops as Roxanne locks onto her.

She manages to get out one word. "Muse!"

I expect the woman who once killed a muse to lick her chops. But she starts to back up, eyes wide with fear, as Roxanne moves toward her with me still holding her hand.

Jake gets out of the way as Cruise backs into the couch, unable to say anything as she falls back onto it. Roxanne is laser-focused on her. The Senator's face begins to twitch, then her whole body starts shaking. She's unable to break Roxanne's hypnotic stare. Her jaw trembles and then she lets out a blood curdling scream.

Rox doesn't react, doesn't let up. She leans over her, goes nose to nose.

Cruise's eyes bug out, filled with terror. Her jaw trembles again. She opens it to scream.

And nothing comes out.

She tries again and is still silent. Cruise grabs her own throat as she realizes her worst fear.

She's now a mute siren.

And then she passes out.

Roxanne blinks and her body relaxes. "It's done."

I wrap my arms around her. "You did it. Thank God you're okay."

"*We* did it," she says. "We flat out fried the bitch. Honestly, Jillian, once I got into her subconscious I realized she would have kicked my ass without your help. She was incredibly powerful. But her voice is gone and so are her powers as a siren."

"For good?"

"Yeah. Just like in the myth, though she also became deaf, which wasn't in the myth."

"What about her powers as a dream weaver?"

Roxanne shakes her head. "No clue. I was totally focused on her abilities as a siren. Anyway, we got a bonus."

"What's that?"

"While I was in her head, I found out what we need to pull the plug on the ID card program. Unfortunately it doesn't make any sense."

"What doesn't make sense?"

"Something about a football."

Chapter 17

Fuzzball yanks open the connecting door to the hotel suite and waves us toward our room. "Get in here, fast!"

"What?" I ask.

"Security's coming. People heard her scream. Move! Now!"

I hear the ding of the elevator, followed by quick footsteps. Roxanne, Jake and I dash into the adjoining room. Fuzzball grabs the room service cart, pulls it into our room, slams the connecting door shut and locks it. We all gather around the monitors.

I place my hand on Roxanne's shoulder. "You feel okay? Any after effects?"

She smiles at me. "You kidding? Never better."

We see two large men in security uniforms rush into the room. One moves quickly to the unconscious Senator, crouches down and takes her pulse. "She's alive," he says to the other guard. "Get the paramedics. Hurry."

The other rent-a-cop keys his two-way radio. "Need medical assistance right now in the suite. It's Senator Cruise."

Thirty minutes later Fuzzball returns from the suite. Cruise was taken out on a stretcher. "I didn't find anything in the room except her carry-on bag and her other outfit."

"So you think her mother always told her to wear nice underwear in case she ended up in the hospital?" asks Roxanne, lightening the mood.

"Not sure if a thong qualifies," I say.

Ryan starts to laugh. "I just thought of something. Wonder what the emergency room people will think of her dominatrix getup?"

"If the media gets there before her staff, she'll be on the front page of The Post," says Jake. "Can you imagine the headline?"

"Gives new meaning to the term Senate Majority Whip," cracks Fuzzball. "Speaking of the media, I think I'll give a reporter friend of mine a head's up. I'm sure he'd love a sleazy lead story." Fuzzball whips out his cell phone and calls a reporter, giving him the details with a gleam in his eye. "Yeah. Everything but a whip and handcuffs." He smiles and hangs up, slipping his cell back into his pocket. "Okay, the lurid tales of Mistress Cruise are underway and will be required reading for all New Yorkers tomorrow." He turns to Roxanne. "And now that we're done with that, let's get back to our other problem. Tell me again what you saw regarding the ID program."

"I didn't see anything physical, I just picked up that thought. That the football was somehow critical to the program. It's the on and off switch. I realize it doesn't make any sense but it was a very powerful thought."

"You're right, it doesn't make sense," says Fuzzball.

"Could be another one of my father's code words," I say.

"But it's not biblical, like the other codes," says Ryan. "We'll figure it out eventually."

"We'd better figure it out quick," says Jake. "We still don't know if Rox affected her powers as a dream weaver. We're not out of the woods yet. She'll probably retaliate if she still has the power."

"True," says Fuzzball, "but she won't be taking out any more muses. And she won't be a very effective Senator without her ability to control the men in Congress and the media with her voice."

Two days later we're not sure what to think. Cruise is out of the hospital and hasn't retaliated, though the tabloids had a field day with her leather outfit, as Fuzzball's contact snapped a photo when she was being treated in the emergency room. Roxanne may or may not have canceled her powers as a dream weaver, or the Senator may be plotting something. But at least her days as a siren are definitely over. And her credibility with voters has taken a serious shot with the photo that went viral and became a hanging curve ball for late night comedians. Her days in politics are definitely numbered, if nothing else.

Meanwhile, news reports on the Senator that are not focused on her after hours hobby as a dominatrix center on her "unexplained loss of hearing and speech" which has the best doctors in the country baffled. Her vocal chords have completely atrophied and cannot be restored. Cruise is soldiering on, communicating through her computer and press secretary. It's obvious she's not going away, but she's lost a serious amount of clout in Congress, especially with the men.

The rest of the news is dominated by what we know to be the effect of the ID cards. Crime is up, people are quitting their jobs in droves, the have-nots are stealing from the haves. The economic playing field is being leveled, and not in a good way. About the only growth industries are security systems and guns.

And we still haven't figured out how the word "football" figures into the whole thing. Nothing in the computer files I stole mentions it, so Sebastien's plan is to get a mind reader into Cruise's head to figure it out. There's no way to get Ryan close enough and so far The Council hasn't been able to get anyone in a one-on-one situation with her. We may have to use my abilities as an amplifier to do it from a distance, but right now she's basically in hiding.

"Jillian! Get down here!" Mom's voice cuts through my deep thoughts and I bound down the stairs.

"What?"

She points at the television.

My eyes widen as I read the graphic across the bottom of the screen.

Senator Cruise dead

"What the hell happened?" I ask.

"She was crossing the street, a car ran the red light and since she couldn't hear she didn't know it was coming. It ran her over and killed her instantly."

My jaw drops as I plop down onto the couch and watch the video which shows a body covered by a white sheet in the middle of a Manhattan street.

Mom wraps an arm around my shoulders, pulls me close and kisses the side of my head. "The dream weaver's dead, Jillian. She can't hurt my little girl anymore. The bitch is gone forever."

Yeah.

And so is the information about how to turn off the ID card.

A few hours later the ring of my cell phone jolts me out of a deep sleep. I crack one eye open and the screen tells me it's Fuzzball. The clock tells me it's two in the morning.

I lean up on one elbow and grab the phone. "Hello?" My voice is filled with gravel.

"Sorry to wake you, Jillian, but this is important."

"It's okay. You need me to save someone?"

"More like the whole planet. Wake up your Mom and get a pot of coffee going."

I sit up and stretch my eyes open. "Why, what's going on?"

"I figured out what the football is. And you need to go back to Cruise's house to find out if I'm right."

"Now? In the middle of the night?"

"As soon as possible. This might be our only chance."

Mom pours the detective a cup of coffee as he enters the kitchen while I work on my second cup. A quick hot shower and the java have me sufficiently in my body. Of course, I'll shortly be out of my body. Quite the caffeine paradox, if you ask me.

"So, don't keep me in suspense," I say. "What is it?"

"It's a briefcase. Or a computer. Or a computer built into a briefcase. I projected myself into her home and saw what I think it might be."

"You *think*? I thought you said you *knew* what it was?"

Fuzzball nods. "I'm almost sure. I was up late last night watching one of those history channels, and this show was talking about Air Force One and how the President always has access to nuclear launch codes and the ability to fire missiles when he's away from the White House. Because of a portable device that controls everything. Anyway, it turns out there's always one designated Secret Service guy with the President who carries a briefcase called the football. Inside the case is the computer that gives the President the ability to fire nukes. Or to fire them and then disarm them. The point is, the football is the key."

"That doesn't mean Cruise's football is the same thing," says Mom.

"I know, but it makes sense and it's worth checking out," he says. "If I'm right and there's a device that will disarm the whole ID card system, we could simply turn it off. Anyway, Jillian needs to get in her house tonight before everyone descends on it tomorrow for funeral plans and the usual vultures start circling for valuables. If I'm right, we've only got one chance to do this, and it's tonight. If there is a version of the President's football in her home, we need to find it before one of her minions does. I'm sure she's not the only one who knows about it. There's got to be her second in command or someone with the ability to use the thing."

The detective has a gleam in his eye that I recognize as one he wears after a big arrest. "You're really pretty sure about this, aren't you?"

Fuzzball reaches across the table and takes my hands. "Look, Jillian, your father's background was in technology and everything he and his followers have done has technology as a central component. It would make sense that Cruise has some sort of master control device either in her Senate office or at home. I've been to the Senate office and didn't see anything that fits. It's got to be what I saw in her house. And since I couldn't open it, you have to."

"So what's the plan?"

"We're going to drive over there and you'll project yourself from my car."

"And when I get in, what then?"

"Open it up. See what's inside. If it looks like some sort of electronic on and off switch, walk it out of there and we'll drive it over to The Council."

It's three in the morning when we pull up to Cruise's home. It's dark and hopefully no one's inside like the last time. The streets are quiet and shiny from a brief shower a few hours ago. A full moon provides plenty of light on what is now a crystal clear night.

Fuzzball kills the car engine and turns to face me. "Okay, it's in her office. There should be enough light from the streetlight and the moon so you can see it. It's a silver box about the size of a briefcase. Slide the chair back from the desk and you'll see it under the desk."

I nod, keeping a close eye on the windows of the home to see if there's any movement. There is none. "Okay, then what?"

"Then open it. If it looks like what I described or some sort of master control device, we'll need to get it out of the house. And if it's locked and you can't open it, we still need it."

"How can I just walk out of there? Surely she has an alarm system."

"You are correct, young lady. And just as surely, I have the code to turn it off as I saw her use it the last time I was there spying on her. Seventeen seventy six."

"My, how appropriate."

"Well, it is a revolution. Though I'm sure our founding fathers would not approve of her objective."

Fuzzball takes another look at the home. It's still dark. "Okay, off you go. Remember, don't turn on the lights and be as quiet as possible just in case."

"Copy that, detective." I nod and close my eyes, focusing on the office I've visited before.

And then I'm there.

There's enough light pouring through the window to see. But what I hear stops me dead in my tracks.

The sound of loud snoring coming from the bedroom on the first floor.

I'm not alone.

My pulse spikes and I consider heading back to my own body but I'm this close, and hopefully I'm not too late. I tiptoe across the office behind the desk. Thankfully the desk chair is on rubber casters, so I gently pull it back. It rolls silently across the hardwood floor.

A glint of silver underneath the desk reflects the light from outside.

The snoring is still strong and steady.

I take a deep breath in an effort to slow my heartbeat, but it doesn't work.

I sit in the chair, lean down, grab the case by the handle and gently lay it flat on top of the desk. There are two snaps holding it closed, same as any standard briefcase. Is it locked? I gently slide one release button while holding the snap with my thumb.

It opens.

I slowly let the first snap spring back so that it doesn't make a sound, then do the same with the other side. I listen carefully for any change in the snoring. There is none.

I gently open the case.

What I see makes my eyes grow wide.

It's Fuzzball's football, all right, with two large buttons. One green marked "enable" and one red marked "disable."

The green button is lit.

But the scary part is the digital counter above the buttons.

It reads more than seventy million and the numbers are heading higher at a fast rate.

It obviously represents the number of people who are connected by the ID cards.

I hit the disable button. It lights up and the numbers freeze. Now all I need to do is walk it out the front door. I remember the creaky steps from my first visit and know it won't be easy. I might have to actually slide down the banister—

A loud cough from the first floor makes me jump and hit my knee hard on the underside of the desk.

I clamp my hand over my mouth as pain shoots up my leg. But that's not what worries me.

Did the sound travel enough to alert whoever is in the house?

A light goes on and illuminates the hallway.

Whoever is in the house heard me.

"You hear something upstairs?" says a woman.

I hear the creak of a mattress, then footsteps heading across the hardwood floor. Another light goes on, the hallway is bright now.

Someone is walking up the steps.

There's no way for me to get the briefcase out of there. The windows don't open so I can't simply toss it out. And whoever is coming up the stairs can just as easily turn on the enable key.

The only option is to destroy the computer and this is my only chance. But I can't simply smash it.

Then I remember what happened to Jake's laptop.

And what will kill any computer, regardless of how sophisticated it might be.

The steps get closer.

I look up at the ceiling and what I need is thankfully there.

I reach across the desk, grab the State of Liberty cigarette lighter, flick it, move to the far end of the office and set the curtains on fire.

They go up like a torch with an audible *whoosh*.

Flames start leaping up the wall and smoke beings to fill the room.

The steps get faster. "Fire!"

I get up on a chair and hold the flame up against the sprinkler head.

An ear-piercing alarm goes off as the sprinkler system engages and it starts to rain in the office.

The water hits the laptop, a few sparks shoot out and the screen goes dark.

I disappear just as the light in the office turns on.

The words I've longed to hear greet me as I enter the kitchen at two in the afternoon after a long nap.

"It's over," says Sebastien. He's seated at the kitchen table, sipping a soda while Fuzzball sits across from him with a beer.

"Really?" I say.

Sebastien nods. "When you shorted out the main control, the whole ID system went down."

I move to the fridge and get some orange juice. "You sure it's down for good?"

"Yes. Our technical staff says the control device was necessary for it to function. The activation system we have at The Summit no longer works."

Fuzzball gets up and gives me his chair. "My friend from the fire department grabbed the football for me. It was fried and fairly melted but there was enough left for the geek squad to analyze it."

Sebastien takes a brownie from a plate on the table. "Yes, and now we know how they incorporated your father's engrams into the technology. So if they try that trick again, we'll know how to defeat it."

"Terrific," I say, taking a sip of juice.

"I must say, Jillian, that was very quick thinking on your part to set the place on fire," says Sebastien.

I smile as I sit down. "I remembered Jake spilling a soda on his laptop and shorting it out. I knew I needed liquid and when I saw the place had a sprinkler system I figured setting it off would do the trick. Thank goodness Cruise was a smoker and had that big lighter on her desk." I turn and look up at the detective. "Did you find out who was inside?"

He shakes his head. "They must have gone out the back door. And they probably won't be back since the place is a total loss. It doesn't really matter. We cut off the head of the snake."

"Yeah," I say. "But what worries me is that there are still followers out there."

Chapter 18

Once again, all is right with the universe. And once again, my friends and I have saved the world as we know it.

But I'm not looking for glory, only a normal life free of threats to take down society.

It's great that it's over and Ryan and I can go out in public again. No more crazy dreams, no more pod people with eye twitches, no more worrying about a siren killing my best friend. It's freezing cold but I don't care. Just walking down the sidewalk holding his hand, even with gloves on, makes it a perfect day. Just life the way it was meant to be for an average eighteen year old girl.

And it doesn't hurt that I'm in love and can fully concentrate on my relationship with the right guy. Our strides are in step, just like our lives. He lets go of my hand and wraps one arm around my shoulder, then pulls me close and kisses me. He doesn't have to say anything.

His look says it all.

"Hey, Jillian!"

I turn toward the voice and see Aspen cross the street, waving at me as she heads in our direction.

"Hi, Aspen." We stop walking, waiting for her to arrive. She smiles at me, then Ryan, and I realize they've never been introduced. "Ryan, this is Aspen. Aspen, my boyfriend Ryan."

She shakes his hand. "Nice to finally meet you, Ryan. I've heard so much about you."

"Likewise," he says.

"You've got a great girl there." She turns back to me. "Hey, Jillian can you spare five minutes?"

"Why, what's up?"

"Well... Trip's taking me on a Caribbean cruise during the Christmas holidays. I can only pack one formal outfit and can't decide. I want to wear something that will knock his socks off. Would you mind coming up to my place and help me choose?"

Ryan rolls his eyes and she notices. She gently touches his forearm. "Don't worry, Ryan, there are only two outfits so it really *will* only take five minutes. This won't be an all day affair."

"Okay," he says. "I was afraid this might turn into a review of an entire closet."

"I live right up the street," she says. "Two blocks. C'mon."

She leads us for a couple of blocks to an impressive townhouse. We climb the stairs as I realize she must be rich. "Nice place."

"Luckily my parents are never here," she says, as she puts a key in the door and leads us inside. "It beats the hell out of living in a dorm."

Trip is sitting at a desk working on a laptop. He gets up to greet us. "Ah, you must be Ryan," he says, smiling as he extends a hand. He's shirtless in a pair of jeans. Kind of an unusual choice for December, but Aspen obviously picks out his wardrobe. Or lack thereof. "I've heard so much about you from Jillian."

His comments strike me as odd since they've met before, though under very uncomfortable circumstances. Maybe Trip is trying for a fresh start. I know Ryan isn't wild about this and seeing Trip's incredible physique will make him feel inadequate all over again. But he puts on a brave face, sticks his hand out to shake. Instead Trip bends down, wraps his arms around Ryan's and lifts him up into a bear hug.

My jaw drops. "What the hell?" I start to move toward them

but Aspen grabs me from behind and yanks my arms behind my back. Ryan grimaces as Trip begins to squeeze him. "What are you doing? Stop it! Let him go!"

"No," says Aspen, who has a tight grip on my arms and pulls me back. "You need to see what it's like when someone you care about gets hurt."

Trip has Ryan's arms pinned against his sides and tightens the grip around his chest. Ryan starts to yell in pain. His legs kick as he tries to escape but they find nothing but air as he's a foot off the floor.

I'm in anguish watching Ryan being hurt while trying to process why he's being attacked. "Why are you doing this?"

But I already know there's only one logical answer.

They work for Cruise.

I twist my body, desperately try to get away from Aspen, but she's so much taller and stronger I can't get free. "Let me go!"

"Stop fidgeting. You're not going anywhere. Crank it up, Trip."

Trip squeezes Ryan harder and his scream goes right through my heart. "Trip, stop it, you're hurting him!"

"That's the idea," says Aspen. She leans forward and speaks directly into my ear. "Now watch."

"I'm teaching him a lesson," says Trip, shooting me a sinister grin. His shoulder muscles twitch as he crushes my boyfriend. Ryan groans, his face twists in pain.

And I can't do a thing to help him.

"Can't... breathe," Ryan says, his voice barely audible. He's quickly getting weaker and is powerless to break free. Trip is smiling at him, obviously enjoying himself as he effortlessly dominates Ryan without even breaking a sweat. He has such a huge size advantage that Ryan doesn't have a chance. His eyes begin to droop as his leg kicks are now slow, without any force behind them. Ryan's chest is swallowed up by Trip's massive arms.

The realization of what's happening brings a flood of tears. "That's enough! Let him go! Trip, I'm begging you! Please let him go!" I start to sob as I see Ryan gasping for air. "Please..."

"Wrap it up, Trip, she's getting hysterical," says Aspen. "And you're just toying with him."

"Aw, c'mon, Aspen. A little longer."

"Can't you see he's done? Finish him!"

"Fine." He looks at Ryan, who is fading and has no fight left in him. His legs have stopped moving and are hanging straight down. "Goodnight, sweet prince."

Oh my God, he's going to kill Ryan! "Nooooo!"

Trip's huge biceps flex and the veins on his arms bulge out as he tightens his clench and leans back, raising Ryan higher in the air. Ryan lets out a moan of pure agony as his eyes bug out, his look one I've never seen.

Absolute fear.

He locks eyes with me as Trip crushes the life out of him.

He knows he's going to die.

My emotions explode. "Stop it!"

Trip closes his eyes and lets out a primitive grunt as his arm and shoulder muscles quickly contract giving Ryan a violent squeeze. Ryan's head jerks back as his face contorts into a silent scream. His legs go straight out and twitch as Trip puts everything he's got into the bear hug. Then Ryan's head falls forward, eyes closed, as his whole body goes limp.

"Oh my God! Ryan!" My knees buckle as my emotions go out of control.

I know the love of my life is dead.

Chapter 19

"You killed him," I say, through uncontrollable sobs. "You bastard."

Trip flashes an evil smile at Aspen, then nods. "Tell her."

"Oh, stop it, Jillian," says Aspen. "He just passed out. You're such a drama queen."

Trip straightens up, relaxes his grip and studies Ryan's face. "Yeah, lover boy is still breathing."

Hope shoots through my veins like adrenaline.

He's alive!

A ray of light.

I try to wrestle my body away again from Aspen but my emotions have drained me and she's still maintaining a strong grip.

Focus, Jillian.

He's alive! You can heal him.

But you have to get to him first.

"Dammit, let me go to him! He's hurt!"

"Not yet," says Aspen. "Trip hasn't finished exercising. He's just warming up."

"I dunno, Aspen, he's not much of a workout," says Trip, now casually holding Ryan up with only one arm. "Too small. Too weak." He lets Ryan's body slide down, lowering his feet to the floor for a moment, then bends over, puts his back against Ryan's waist and effortlessly hoists my boyfriend over his shoulder. Ryan is like a rag doll bent in half over one shoulder, arms hanging limp to the floor. Trip has one arm wrapped tightly around his legs while he flexes his free arm in some sort of victory pose. "I'll finish him off later."

"Please don't hurt him anymore! Please!"

"Like I said, I'm teaching him a lesson. He needs to stay away from you. You're mine now."

I glare at him. "I'll never be yours."

"Well, then," says Aspen, "I guess you can watch Trip crush what's left of your boyfriend when he wakes up. You only saw a little taste of what he's capable of. Face it, Jillian, this is no contest. I mean, look at this."

Trip is showing off, now sipping a soda as he parades around the room with Ryan draped over his shoulder like he weighs nothing. "The bigger and stronger survive, Jillian. It's the law of nature. Soon as he wakes up, round two."

"And you're gonna watch him snap Ryan like a twig," says Aspen. "Unless..."

I have to get to Ryan.

"Okay, okay, I'll do whatever you want, just let him go and don't hurt him. Put him down, Trip, you've made your point. I get it. You're a lot stronger than Ryan. I give up. I'm yours. Now please put him down. I'll do anything you want if you don't hurt him anymore."

"Smart decision," says Aspen. "You just saved his life."

Trip moves toward a couch and dumps Ryan on it. He's still unconscious.

Aspen finally lets me go and I run to Ryan. Tears are streaming down my face as I take his head in my hands. Thankfully he's still breathing, but barely. "Hang in there, Ryan. I love you." My voice cracks as I take Ryan's hand and send some healing power into him.

"Payback is hell, huh?" says Aspen.

I turn to face her. "Payback? For what? I thought we were friends."

"Friends? Pffft. Jillian, you are *soooo* naive."

"Answer the question, Aspen. Payback for what? What did I ever do to you?"

"It's what you did to my parents, Jillian. Last spring you turned my dad into a vegetable and now you took my mother's powers. Which cost mom her life."

My eyes widen while my jaw drops.

She locks eyes with me with a look that is pure evil, and smiles. "Look, Trip, she just figured it out. I knew the girl was smart. Yeah, sweetie, Rebecca Cruise was my mother and J.T. Decker's my dad. So how ya doin'... *sister*?"

I gently stroke Ryan's hair as I continue healing him. Trip has left me alone with him while he and Aspen are talking in another room. Ryan's breathing is still labored, but getting stronger. He's unconscious. I lift up his shirt and see his chest is seriously bruised, the sight of which makes me tear up again.

I'm too upset and having trouble concentrating. Focus, Jillian.

I wipe my tears with my free hand and send as much life force as I can into his body. It may knock me out, but I have to save him. Then we can live to fight another day.

I feel a bit weaker but remain conscious as my energy flows into him. Ryan's breathing gradually improves and his eyes flicker open. "What happened?" he whispers.

"Shhhh. Don't talk. Let me concentrate."

He tries to sit up but grimaces in pain and grabs his side. "Ow. I think he broke a couple of my ribs."

"Shhh. They're in the other room." I close my eyes, focus harder, see his bruised body healing itself. A few minutes later I open my eyes to find his are open and he's smiling. "That's good, Sparks. I'm fine now. What the hell happened?"

I lift up his shirt and see the bruises have disappeared. I tell him the quick version, his eyes bugging out when he finds out Aspen is my half sister.

"So what do they want?" he whispers.

"Trip wants me. If I don't agree to leave you for him he'll..." I bite my lower lip as the tears flow again. "I'm sorry, Ryan, I have no choice. You'll have to let me go."

"Not gonna happen, Sparks."

"Ryan, he's too strong! He almost killed you. I won't let him hurt you again and next time he *will* kill you. You have to stay away from me. For now anyway, until we figure out how to defeat him."

"You said they're in the other room?"

"Yeah. They figured we weren't going anywhere with you hurting so badly."

"You got any juice left?"

"Yeah, plenty. You still hurt?'

"No, I'm fine. I need a boost to read their minds. Give me a jump."

Five minutes later he opens his eyes. I let go of his hand.

"Okay, I got both of them."

"And?"

"I know his weakness. We can beat him, but we can only do it together."

"Okay, how?"

He tells me he needs an ID card before going back into Trip's mind and that I need to get help.

I furrow my brow. "An ID card? How exactly will this work?"

We hear Trip and Aspen coming. "No time to explain. Now go get Rox and Jake. Oh, and bring two sets of earplugs."

"Huh?"

"Aspen is a siren, like her mother. Jake and I will need protection from her."

"Does she also have the abilities of a dream weaver like her mother?"

He shakes his head. "Cruise wasn't the dream weaver. She was just a siren."

"She wasn't the dream weaver?"

"Nope. You're not gonna believe this."

"What?"

"Trip is the dream weaver."

Ryan plays dead as Trip and Aspen walk back into the room.

"See, he's still breathing," says Aspen.

I glare at her. "Get on with it, Aspen. I'm willing to make a deal on three conditions. You promise not to hurt him anymore. You let me go get some help for Ryan. He's seriously hurt and needs medical attention. And you answer a few questions. After that, I'm yours."

"I could carry him down to the hospital," says Trip, smiling.

"No, they'll ask too many questions about what happened to him," says Aspen. "You don't need to be involved. Anyway, Jillian, I agree to your conditions. Ryan won't be touched as long as you keep your part of the bargain and give yourself to Trip. And I don't have a problem with you going anywhere because you have to come back."

"But no tricks or Ryan faces the consequences," says Trip.

"As I said before, you made your point. I know what you're capable of."

He glares at me. "Actually, you have no idea."

"Okay, Trip, I think she got the message," says Aspen. She turns back to me. "As for questions..."

"What the hell, Aspen, it's not like it's gonna help her," says Trip. "Fire away."

"Fine," she says.

"First of all, I thought you guys were my friends."

"You are so easily played and incredibly naive," says Aspen. "You're brilliant, but innocent."

"I won't argue with you there. But, Trip, why do you want me if you have Aspen?"

"It's our destiny for you and me to be together. Among other things. And I really do find you incredibly attractive. I know you feel the same way, so don't deny it. I see the way you look at me."

"But don't you love Aspen?"

Aspen chuckles a bit. "Jillian, Trip and I are just part of the team. You needed to believe we were in love. You have to admit it made you jealous, which was our intent. When I was talking about women staring at him at the Halloween party, I was talking about you. Your crush on Trip was beyond obvious. But our relationship was an act."

"But I saw you two in the reading. In my crystal ball."

Aspen smiles. "You saw what the dream weaver wanted you to see. You never actually did a reading for me."

Trip cocks his head at Aspen. "Her mother wanted her to mate with someone who had superior powers. That would be me."

I do my best to tighten my face. "You have powers?"

He nods. "Hi, Trip Logan. Dream weaver."

I feign shock so well they both smile. They buy it. I turn to Aspen. "Your mother wasn't—"

"Nope, she wasn't a dream weaver. Just a plain old siren, but a very powerful one at that. Or she was until you stole her powers that led to her death. You murdered my mother, Jillian." Aspen's voice quivers.

"She was killed in an accident."

"As a result of your actions."

"She murdered a muse, did you know that? Or does killing a beautiful person not constitute a crime in your mind?"

Aspen shrugs. "Ancient history, and muses are of no consequence. But back to the present. She figured that since I carried the genes from our father as well as her own that producing a child with a dream weaver would create someone with incredible powers. Powers that would dominate anything else, powers never before seen. Perhaps even a new power. And it doesn't hurt that Trip's a perfect physical specimen, to which you can personally attest."

My face tightens. "So you two are... some sort of Adam and Eve lab experiment to create a super race? Ewwww."

"Jillian, don't take the romance out of it," says Aspen. "It's not like we haven't been enjoying trying. I mean, look at him. Imagine what it's like getting physical with Trip." She playfully slaps her face. "Oh, wait, I forgot. You've done that already and I'm told you enjoyed it a great deal."

I turn to Trip. "So it was *you* who manipulated my dreams."

He nods. "Guilty as charged. I needed to lay the groundwork to make you infatuated. I even made you step into traffic so I could rescue you. I needed to start a relationship with you to make the dream become reality... that you desperately want me and we're meant to be together."

"You expect me to feel that way after what you just did to Ryan?"

He flashes a smile. "Jillian, I'll be taking charge of both your dreams and your waking life. You won't even remember Ryan ever existed, like you didn't remember him when we first kissed. You'll spend a happy life with me, living in that home I created in your dream. Remember how much you enjoyed that last one? This time, no alarm clocks to interrupt us. You'll think you're living a perfectly normal life, only I'll be controlling it. I've give you everything you want, Jillian. When you're awake and when you're sleeping. And I think you'll agree we do have incredibly physical chemistry."

"Don't flatter yourself."

"Trust me, Jillian, you'll enjoy it," says Aspen. "He's quite skillful in the bedroom."

My face tightens again, the thought of being physical with Trip now sickening me. "So, you just want to keep me in some dream state box for the rest of my life? Living in a fake reality like a Stepford wife?"

Aspen shakes her head. "Again, too innocent."

"I don't understand."

"You're a powerful seer and carry your father's genes as well," she says. "Jillian, you're lab experiment number two."

They think I'm going out to get help for Ryan.

I'm going to get help, but of a different kind. And when I return, it will be my double.

Aspen heads for the door. "I'll be back later, Trip. And if she doesn't come back, you can do whatever you want to her boyfriend. Have fun."

"I'll be back," I say, getting up from the couch. "Don't you dare touch him."

"By the way," says Trip, "just so you don't think I'm totally heartless, I'll be happy to wipe any memories of you from his mind as well. So you won't have to think about him missing you."

"I'll be happy to take care of his needs," says Aspen. "I wasn't kidding when I called him hot. So don't worry your pretty little head that he'll be lonely. Trip will make sure he's infatuated with me."

My eyes narrow as my jaw clenches. I want to slap the bitch, but need to focus on the task.

"You guys ready?" I ask, as I stop in front of Aspen's door.

Jake and Roxanne nod. "Let's rock," says Rox, as she cracks her knuckles.

I knock on the door and Trip quickly answers. "Well, if it isn't Jillian and her merry band. What are *they* doing here?"

"I said I was going to get help for Ryan, or did you already forget? He's in no condition to get home by himself, thanks to you."

"You didn't say you were bringing people with powers."

"They're my closest friends. And you didn't specify who I could bring."

He nods. "Fine. But no tricks or he'll be the one to pay." He cracks his knuckles for effect. "And I won't go easy on him this time."

"I'm honoring my part of the deal. They won't do anything but take him to the hospital. I don't want him hurt anymore."

Aspen thankfully hasn't returned. We move past Trip to the couch where Ryan is grimacing, pretending to be in pain. "Hey,

Sparks."

"I told him about our agreement," says Trip. "So say your goodbyes and get him out of here. Make it quick."

I sit on the edge of the couch and hug Ryan as tears roll down my cheeks. It feels so real I don't have to pretend. "I love you, babe." I lean forward and hug him.

"Ow, not too hard," he says. "I'm real sore."

I lean back and smooth his hair out of his face, then lock eyes with him. "I'll always love you, Ryan."

"Same here, Sparks. I'll never forget you." He kisses me like never before, like it really is a last kiss, sending a bolt of electricity through my body and distracting me from the task at hand.

"Wrap it up before I go into a diabetic coma," says Trip.

"God, you're an ass," says Roxanne.

"Watch your mouth, muse. A siren will be back here any minute and she eats your kind for lunch."

Roxanne backs off, though I can tell from her clenched fists she'd like to wind up and kick the guy in the balls. Jake glares at Trip but knows better than to take on a guy twice his size. She and Jake move toward Ryan, get on both sides of him and help him up as he stretches his arms over their shoulders.

Then Jake points a finger across the room. He makes a glass vase fall off a shelf and crash.

The sound makes Trip whip his head around. "What the hell?"

I pull out the ID card from my pocket as Ryan stands up on his own, straight and tall. I move closer to him, ready to give him more power. I expect him to start executing his plan, but he goes rogue.

"Hey, Trip," he says.

My eyes widen. *What the hell are you doing? Start going into his mind!*

Trip turns around just as Ryan's hand balls into a fist and flies toward him in a blur, lightning fast, so fast I can't believe it, catching him square on the jaw. Trip's eyes roll back in his head, then he falls back like a tree and hits the floor with a thud. He's out cold.

"Nobody messes with my girl," says Ryan, shaking his hand.

My jaw drops. "Ryan, how the hell—"

"Later, Sparks. We gotta move. Gimme the card."

I hand him the card as he crouches down next to Trip, who has a huge red welt on his chin and a couple of teeth next to him on the floor. Blood is oozing out of his mouth and a pool is forming from the back of his head. Ryan places his thumb on the ID card, then takes Trip's hand and turns to me.

"Now, Sparks. Gimme all you got. Crank it, babe."

I kneel down, put my hands on his shoulders and focus, sending energy into his body.

Ryan closes his eyes.

Trip's instantly open wide.

Filled with fear.

"He's awake!" I say.

"Focus, Sparks!"

I expect Trip to get up and fight, but instead his body begins to twitch. Ryan maintains his grip on one hand while still holding the ID card. Trip's free hand goes to his head as he screams in mortal agony, a sound I've heard before.

When we fried my father's brain.

Trip's eyes bug out as his body goes into violent convulsions. I continue to send energy into Ryan as he hangs on to Trip's hand.

And then it's over.

Trip's body seems to melt into the floor as he exhales. His breathing stops, his eyes open, staring into space.

"Oh my God! Is he..."

Ryan nods as he lets go of Trip's hand and stands up.

"You killed him?" I ask, looking up at him.

He's still looking at Trip. "Nope. Your father did."

"Huh?"

"I'll explain later." He gets up and looks down at Trip with disdain. "One down, one to go." He extends a hand and helps me up, giving me a deadly serious look I've never seen. Like a soulless gunslinger in an old western. He gently runs his hand over the side of my face. "Like I said, nobody messes with my girl."

I'm trying to process the cold, calculating Ryan I've never known when I hear the key in the door and the doorknob turn. "Here she comes."

Ryan and I are standing over Trip, who is lifeless on the floor in an expanding pool of blood. Jake and Roxanne run to the other room and peek around the corner.

The guys quickly put in their earplugs.

The door opens and Aspen's face drops immediately as she takes in the scene. "Oh my God, Trip!" She runs to him and kneels down, taking his face in her hands. She leans her head against his chest. "He's not breathing!"

"That's generally the case when you're dead," says Ryan, without a hint of emotion.

She whips her head around and glares at me. "What did you do?" she asks in a guttural tone.

"My boyfriend kicked his ass," I say, casually, patting Ryan on the shoulder. "Taught him a lesson. I think he got the point. Somehow I don't think there'll be a *round two*. He'd carry him out but you can take out the trash yourself."

"You're gonna pay for this—"

"Hey Aspen, think fast!" Jake's voice makes her turn around as he sends a marble paperweight flying into her forehead. She drops to the floor, next to Trip, unconscious.

Aspen is stretched out on the floor, flat on her back, still out cold with a small red welt near her hairline. Roxanne is straddling her, sitting on her stomach. Jake has a death grip on her wrists while Ryan holds her ankles. I'm kneeling next to Roxanne, a bit weary from helping Ryan but amazingly I still have enough juice left for one more round.

Roxanne playfully slaps Aspen's face. "Wake uuuuppppp," she says, like a mom rousing a small child. "C'mon, earth to Aspen.

C'mon, honey, we're gonna have a sing-along. Let's do Kumbaya."

Aspen's eyes flicker open, then widen quickly as she sees Roxanne on top of her. "Muse!"

"That's right. I'm your worst friggin' nightmare. Get ready to be inspired."

Aspen struggles to get away but the guys hold her firm. She cranes her neck and sees them, then looks at Roxanne. "You wanna go? Fine. Then leave the men out of it." She starts to sing a few notes, watching Ryan for a reaction that doesn't come. "What the hell?"

I shake the half-empty bag of earplugs at her. "They can't hear you, Aspen. There's this marvelous new invention called earplugs. Maybe you've heard of it. Or maybe you should have read your Greek mythology and learned how Odysseus beat the system."

She glares at me, then turns to Roxanne. "Fine. Let's go, bitch."

Roxanne gives her the death stare. "Bring it."

Roxanne turns and winks at me while giving me a sly smile. I put my hands on her shoulders and send energy into her body, all I've got. There's no point in saving anything at this point. She turns back to Aspen, then starts to sing what I know is the beginning of her favorite song, *Bad to the Bone*. "Buh-duh-DA-duh-da-DUH."

Aspen's eyes widen in fear as Rox locks onto her and I know she's headed into the girl's subconscious. She maintains her hypnotic stare for about a minute, then Aspen's mouth slowly opens and her head starts to shake. Roxanne remains steady, unmoved, as her eyes focus on the siren. Finally Aspen's entire body begins to tremble and she lets out a loud scream. Just like her mother.

Roxanne doesn't stop staring at her. She's still locked in.

Aspen opens her mouth to scream again and nothing comes out. A look of pure terror washes over her face.

Roxanne relaxes and I know the session is over.

Aspen tries to scream again. She turns to me and tries to talk but her voice is gone.

I cock my head to the side and widen my eyes. "Aw, Aspen,

are you trying to tell me something? Speak up, I can't hear you."

"Let her go," says Roxanne, as tears begin to roll down Aspen's cheeks. "I'm done. And she's done." Ryan and Jake release her.

Aspen clutches her throat.

I put my arm around Roxanne's shoulders as I look at Aspen. "By the way, Aspen, *this* is my sister."

"Her powers are gone?" asks Ryan.

Roxanne nods. "I plucked her feathers and wore 'em like a hat. In her subconscious, I mean. A mute siren is kind of an oxymoron, don't you think? This one can still hear, though." She turns to Aspen. "Hey, maybe you can get a gig as a Central Park mime."

Aspen bites her lip and closes her eyes, sobbing silently.

"So, *Bad to the Bone* did her in, huh?" asks Jake.

She shakes her head and smiles. "Nah, I went with Elton John. I figured *The Bitch is Back* was more appropriate."

The world begins to spin a bit and I feel myself growing faint. "Almost forgot," I say. "Need your cell phone."

Roxanne hands it to me and I call Fuzzball.

"Everyone okay?" he asks.

"Yeah. It's over. Cleanup on aisle five."

"On my way."

I hang up, hand the phone back, exhale and lean back. Giving my energy to both Ryan and Roxanne, along with the incredible emotion of the last few hours, has me exhausted. "Guys, I am seriously fried."

My fumes run out, and the world goes black.

Chapter 20

I hear a hollow voice from what seems to be very far away. "Wake up, sweetie."

A hand touches my shoulder and gently shakes me. My eyes flicker open and I see Mom sitting on the edge of my bed. "Hey, Mom."

"Sleep well?"

"Yeah, like a rock. How long was I out?"

"About a day and a half."

My eyes widen. "Oh my God! I've never been out that long."

"Fuzzball says when you factor emotion into things, it takes longer to recover. Roxanne and Ryan came by and filled me in. After what you've been through, I'm not surprised."

She hands me a glass of juice and I quickly drain it as I'm parched. "So what happened? I mean, after I came back here?"

"Fuzzball made the situation go away. He got Trip's death listed as a cerebral hemorrhage even though it wasn't. He didn't have to do anything to cover up Aspen."

"Why would he have to cover up the fact that she lost her voice?"

"Because she's dead."

"Aspen's dead? What happened?"

"Jumped out of a moving car as they were taking her to The Summit. Got hit by a bus."

I should feel something but I don't. Even though she was a blood relative.

I'm never telling Mom about her relationship to me. The fact that she was the same age as I am confirms that my father was cheating on my mother.

"Anyway," says Mom, "you need to get your ass in gear. Take a shower, do your hair and put on something nice. Sebastien's picking us up in an hour and taking everyone out to dinner."

"Good, I'm starving." I throw back the covers and swing my legs out of bed as Mom starts to leave the room. "Hey, Mom?"

"Yeah, sweetie?"

"I'm a little confused about Ryan. About something that happened when I went back."

"About what?"

"When he took on Trip... went into his mind... and Trip died. It was like Ryan was a different person. I've never seen that side of him. He was, I don't know, almost cold about the whole thing. About the end result. He watched it and didn't even react, showed no emotion at all. Like he was turning off a light."

Mom comes back into my room and takes my shoulders in her hands. "Jillian, the Ryan you grew up with was a boy. He's a man now. And he's a man who protected the woman he loved. He'd do anything for you. He'd do anything not to lose you. And the fellow that died would just as soon have killed you both and not batted an eye."

Nothing quite like lobster for your first meal after you've slept thirty-six hours or so. Breakfast of champions.

The mood isn't festive, but more one of relief. I mean, let's face it, people died. But they were very bad people who would have killed us given the chance. And done God knows what to the rest of the planet.

Sebastien is at the head of the table, while I sit opposite him with Ryan to my right. Roxanne and Jake are on one side of the table while my Mom is next to Fuzzball on the other. I still haven't had the chance to talk to Ryan about what happened and how he managed to take down Trip. Still, I'm fat and happy after my favorite crustacean, a fried calamari appetizer and a huge slice of raspberry cheesecake. Ryan offered to split one but I wanted my own. And then, of course, mom reaches over with her fork, calls "tribute" and steals half of it anyway. Roxanne comments that I'm so obsessed with food I was probably Italian in a previous life.

Sebastien finishes his last bite of cheesecake and places his fork on the plate, then takes a sip of coffee. "I must say, you four young people have renewed my faith in your generation. And Ryan, your bravery and inspiration were nothing short of phenomenal in defeating the dream weaver."

Ryan smiles and nods at Sebastien. "Thank you, Sir. I appreciate that."

"Yes," says Fuzzball, raising a glass in Ryan's direction. "You're not a fireman but you're one of New York's bravest."

"What am I, chopped liver?" asks Roxanne.

"I was about to get to you, young lady," says Sebastien. "Considering the outcome the last time Cruise took on a muse, you are to be commended for putting your life at risk."

"You're the toughest girl I know," says Fuzzball. "Anytime you wanna join the force, let me know. You'd kick ass."

She folds her arms, smiles and nods. "Thank you, that's much better."

"Okay," I say, dabbing my lips and putting my napkin on the table. "Since I've been out cold for a day and a half and everyone else seems to know what happened, how about filling me in?"

Everyone laughs as Ryan turns to me. "Where do you want me to start?"

"You know what I don't understand? Why wouldn't Trip, if he could control everyone's dreams, just make us forget each other like he said he was going to? Why go through the whole thing of attacking you and convincing me to make a deal in order to spare you?"

"Because the one type of paranormal person not affected by a dream weaver is a mind reader. We're immune. When he told you he was going to make me forget you, he lied. He knew he couldn't control my dreams or reality, so he had to make me so afraid that I'd let you go. And threaten to kill me if you didn't go along. I guess he told you that so you'd think I would be risking my life to try and get you back."

"It worked. But how did you come up with the idea of using the ID card?"

"When I read Trip's mind I discovered the weakness of a dream weaver."

"Yeah, you said that, but you didn't have time to tell me what it was. So not being able to control you was the weakness?"

Ryan shakes his head. "No, not at all. That was just a factor of his powers. The weakness was that his mind had to remain pure. He was the one person who couldn't receive any input from anyone else. It was as if his brain had a deadly allergy to any outside force. Reading his mind would have no effect. But adding something to it would be devastating. So even though he was one of your father's minions, ironically he was the one person in the country who could never have an ID card. He was terrified of even touching one of those things."

"Okay. But he never touched it."

"Indirectly, he did. One of the rarely used talents of mind readers is connecting two subjects. Sort of like a go-between for a Vulcan mind meld. Anyway, I connected him with your father's engrams in the ID card. The tech guys at The Summit were pretty sure you could get the engrams by touching it even if the card wasn't activated, which made sense since it was natural to assume not every person who got one in the mail would activate the thing. So I took a shot and it was true. I connected him with the engrams in the card. Once that invaded his brain, it destroyed his ability."

My eyes widen. "Oh my God! That was a hell of a chance you

took."

"That's why he's so brave," says Fuzzball.

"Did you know he would die?"

Ryan shakes his head. "Hell, I didn't even know if it would work. But it was the only shot we had."

I fold my arms. "And speaking of taking chances, you were supposed to go into his mind the minute Jake distracted him by breaking the vase. What was the deal with punching him in the jaw?"

"I figured he'd be easier to deal with if he was unconscious."

"After what he did to you, why did you think you could knock him out?"

"You know those boxing classes I started taking? Well, my instructor tells me I'm a natural, that's he's never seen faster hands. He also told me something about guys who like to get physical. The ones who don't mind getting hit in the head take up boxing. The ones who do mind, go for wrestling. And he said even though a wrestler might have a size advantage, he might also have a glass jaw."

"Might?"

"Yeah. Might."

"Suppose you didn't knock him out?"

"Jillian, I couldn't live without you. If my plan didn't work, I didn't care what he did to me because you'd be out of my life. And he'd take your life from you. We'd both be basically dead anyway."

I bite my lower lip as my eyes begin to well up.

"Okay, that's enough, you two," says Roxanne. "Before I get a cavity."

Thankfully, my food obsession has never been affected by this whole ordeal. The smell of the hot, steaming pizza is making my mouth water as I knock on Ryan's door.

He opens it and smiles. "Well, this is a surprise. Thought you were beaming over later?"

I pull the receipt off the box. "Let's see, you ordered a double supreme, extra cheese. And one redhead wearing a short skirt who's in a romantic mood."

He gives my outfit the once over and scratches his chin as his face scrunches up. "I dunno... the skirt might not be short enough."

"Hey!"

"Get in here." He pulls me in, shuts the door, puts the pizza on a table, takes me in his arms and kisses me.

"I figured it was your last night in the dorm before Christmas, so it might be your last pizza for a while."

"Funny. But we do have pizza at home, you know."

"And it would be our last chance to sleep together."

"That's something we can't get at home. It'll be a rough two weeks."

I lean up and kiss his cheek. "So, come on, let's eat. Pizza's getting cold."

He furrows his brow.

"Yeah, it's the real me. I'm staying for breakfast, too."

Ryan slides into bed shirtless with pajama bottoms. Moonlight spills through the window as a strong winter wind makes the glass vibrate a bit.

"Cold outside," I say, snuggling closer. "You know, down the road when we have a house, I'd love to have a fireplace in the bedroom."

"Great idea. Though you're hot enough."

"Thank you, kind sir. You're not too bad yourself."

I rest my head on his chest and run one hand across his stomach, then up to his shoulder.

And suddenly I feel it. An attraction much stronger than anything I felt with Trip.

The sensation steals my breath. "Oh. My."

He lifts his head and looks at me with concern. "You okay, Sparks?"

I lean up and look into his eyes. "Everything's different now, isn't it?"

"What do you mean?"

"You. Me. Us. It's not the same as it was."

"Is this some sort of redhead logic that needs a translator?"

"No, silly. It's just... you look different to me all of a sudden."

"Yeah, I get that a lot. Must be the haircut."

I rest my chin on his chest. "Stop it, Ryan, I'm trying to be serious.

"I'm sorry. I'm not sure what you're getting at. Is this about sex? You having second thoughts?"

"No. I still want to wait. You okay with that?"

"Sure, no problem. Though sleeping with you raises temptation to another level. But you're my girl, you love me, that's all that matters. I can wait."

"Thank you. I realize it's harder for a guy."

"That is an incredibly poor choice of words, Sparks."

I seriously blush and crack up as I lose my train of thought for a moment. He smiles at me, melts my heart.

"Okay, enough jokes," he says. "So what was on your mind? I can tell something is bothering you."

"We haven't really had a chance to talk about what happened. I mean with Trip."

"I went over it at dinner."

"Not that part. The part before. When he attacked you."

"It hurts to think about it even though you healed me. But if you wanna talk about it, I don't mind. It does have a happy ending."

"Ryan, I wanted to tell you that I only agreed to go with him because he was going to hurt you even more. After you passed out... I totally lost it since I thought you were dead. Then after I found out you weren't he said he was going to finish you off. Considering what he'd already done, I assumed that meant he would kill you. And they were going to make me watch. That's why I agreed. They told me they'd spare you if I gave myself to Trip."

"You don't have to explain yourself, Sparks. You were putting my life before your own."

"It was just so hard to see you being tortured."

"Trust me, it didn't feel real good either. If I could've gotten my hands free I would have punched him. But he was smart pinning my arms like he did and picking me up so I couldn't use my legs."

"*You* were smarter."

"In the end, yeah. But damn, that guy was incredibly strong."

"I still cannot believe you bet it all on one punch. You realize that for the third time this year you risked your life for me. That guy could have killed you."

"Actually, I thought I was dead when Aspen told him to finish me. He gave me this look right before he squeezed me for the last time... this look of pure evil... I really thought he was going to kill me and I knew he had the strength to do it. I was already in serious pain and his grip was so strong around my chest I could barely get any air. And when he leaned back and put his shoulders into it... I felt like I was being crushed by a python. I mean, he broke my ribs with his bare hands. I've never felt so helpless."

I bite my lower lip and my eyes well up a bit. I run my fingers through his hair as I look into his soul. "I really thought I'd lost you, Ryan."

"Well, reports of my death were greatly exaggerated. But I thought I was a goner. I was so close to him I did get a quick glimpse into his mind and saw that he'd once killed a guy by breaking his back."

"And yet after all that you challenged him again. A guy half a foot taller, seventy pounds heavier and incredibly strong."

He smiles and runs his hand across my cheek. "And look who won. David beats Goliath again."

"You know, that gives me an idea for a nickname for you."

"What?"

"Slingshot."

He shrugs. "I'll take it under advisement. By the way, young lady, the next time I tell you I want to get strong for you, please don't argue with me."

I put out my lower lip in a pout and give him my sad little girl look, which I know he can't resist. "Yes, Sir. I'm sorry I was a bad girl."

He shakes his head and smiles. "Dammit, I hate when you go all Strawberry Shortcake on me. You know I can't stay mad at you when you hit me with that."

I shoot him a big smile. "Just my way of controlling you. You may have beaten a guy built like Thor but you're no match for a hundred and fifteen pound redhead."

"I know, and it pisses me off that I'm powerless against you. So fine, you're forgiven. Though I don't expect you to *obey* on anything else."

"You got that right, Mister. But seriously, getting back to what happened, Ryan. After you sent my father's engrams into his mind. There was this side of you I've never seen. You had this look, like, I don't know. A gunslinger. All the rules were off the table. Trip died right in front of us and you didn't blink. It's not like you see people die every day. Or have a hand in it. I never knew you could be so tough. You've always been such a kind, gentle person."

"Jillian, for such a smart girl you sometimes really miss the obvious."

"And that would be?"

"You're worth fighting for and protecting. Regardless of the odds. And when it comes to you, there are no rules and I won't fight fair."

My eyes get misty as I smile and give him a soft kiss, then rest my head back on his chest, listening to his steady heartbeat. Mom's right. The boy I grew up with is now a man.

One worth fighting for.

And what I felt for Trip isn't half of what I feel for Ryan right now. The electricity is off the charts. The dreams that tortured me are gone, erased forever from my memory.

Harder for a guy, my ass.

"You know what, Ryan?"

"What, Sparks?"

"I think I've got things backwards. The hundred and fifteen pound redhead is powerless against *you*."

"About damn time." Ryan reaches over and strokes my hair. "Hey, with all that's been going on I haven't had the chance to do any holiday shopping. So what do you want for Christmas, Sparks?"

I lean up and rest my chin on his chest as I look at him. "Got everything I want right here."